CU01083973

ON REBECCA G

...**The power of this poetic fiction**—a fiction of a very real death—emanates from Goodman's Stein-like maxims which help make sense of what is clearly, in her now fragile world, without sense, without meaning.... Goodman transforms her experiences into a kind of mythic story that also represents her attempts to heal herself...in a kind of magical recovery....Peace and meaning come gradually through language, the very language of Goodman's book....The private sorrow has turned into a public act. This gifted author ends her work in a long prose poem titled "Night Garden," answering, like Molly Bloom, "yes," to the voyage into darkness, a kind of dream garden "full of green."

Douglas Messerli

A book-long, disassembled keen, a reverse index of longing after loss, Rebecca Goodman's spare *Aftersight* is a wonderful achievement. It is connected in its stillness to influences such as the ancient Chinese poets as well as contemporary innovation. Its clarity and dwelling place: consciousness.

Stacey Levine

It would be hard to overstate how thrilled it made me to read Rebecca Goodman's new collection *Aftersight*. As is in her earlier work, *The Surface of Motion*, the writing is always superb—and always deeply compelling.

David St. John

All the echoes of memory and the rapidly disintegrating past come into play in Rebecca Goodman's beautiful meditative novel—a chamber piece for embattled voices that unfolds inside the natural world. The narrator, taking on guises, tries to make sense of what it means to be alive, "these things I can think and feel." Goodman writes at perfect pitch, looking back, looking forward, on the border between holding on and letting go. I couldn't stop reading.

Lewis Warsh

FORGOTTEN NIGHT

Forgotten Night

Rebecca Goodman

SPUYTEN DUYVIL
New York   Paris

Excerpts from *Forgotten Night* first appeared in the *Notre Dame Review, Denver Quarterly, Mantissa, Marginalia*, and *Mad Hatters' Review*.

ISBN 978-1-956005-61-5

Library of Congress Cataloging-in-Publication Data

Names: Goodman, Rebecca, author.
Title: Forgotten night / Rebecca Goodman.
Description: New York City : Spuyten Duyvil, [2022] |
Identifiers: LCCN 2022003609 | ISBN 9781956005615 (paperback)
Subjects: LCGFT: Novels.
Classification: LCC PS3607.O589 F67 2022 | DDC 813/.6--dc23
LC record available at https://lccn.loc.gov/2022003609

For Martin, Leonard, and Victoria

Three times I knocked on the door at 12 rue des Juifs. I waited. The courtyard still. From steep wooden stairs leading to the ramparts, a cat hissed at me. I knocked again.

The stone walls were cracked. Musty. A sign on the stairs warned of danger.

The cat came down a step—out of its steep darkness. I held my hand out to it. It hissed again.

No motion. No wind. The sky above the courtyard grey, almost hidden. I stepped back. The presence of memory shifting inside me.

I stepped back—unable to speak.

A woman pushing a baby stroller walked past. Madame, she stopped. Can I help you?

She didn't move. She repeated, Can I help you? She looked down, lifting the corner of the blue blanket covering the baby carriage.

I could not see the baby. I did not hear a sound. Not a cry, not a breath.

She waited. Unwilling to leave. At once a strange distance between us. What I wanted to reveal to her—but could not. The notion of self—the representation of the body. Blurred moments that erased the space we stood in.

I looked up at the shuttered windows. The empty flowerpots. I thought I heard voices. Laughter. Quickly dissolving into silence. Was there no one left?

I'm looking for Madame Brissac, I said. I think she lives here.

The woman shrugged her shoulders. I don't know, she answered. The name? she asked.

Brissac, I repeated. I believe the family lives here.

I don't know, she answered. She smiled. Pointed to the center of town. Ask in town. Good day, she said.

She opened the door on the far side of the gravel courtyard, entered, then shut the door behind her.

I knocked again. No sound. No response. When I stepped back from the door, I looked up. Words rained all around me. At first a soft drizzle—conjunctions, words that seemed to connect but not describe. And, but, so—and I thought about those words that tried to connect. My childhood. My lined notebook. My awkward print. And then, softly, the words penetrating my clothes, my body. Adverbs, adjectives. Raining down on my skin, beneath my skin. Flowing through me. Disguising me. Revealing me. Forming the notion of who I was and who I could be. When I looked around, I was ensconced in language—a language I could not understand—but feel. Words breaking apart mid-air. Fractured into letters, consonants, vowels. Symbols, punctuation marks. Broken into images, sounds, birdcalls, wind. The water well. The stream. The walls surrounding the village. The silence around me. The landscape of my body. Of my history. Of the courtyard. Foreign—and yet near. Every word that fell on me marked me with a closeness I could almost reach—an impenetrable distance that betrayed me. The distance between.

Time fractured. I looked down. The words dissolved into puddles.

Alone. In the courtyard. The distant sounds in the square beyond.

I stepped back. Waiting, watching for movement. Would the shutters open? The blue paint, peeling, the steep dark stairs leading to the ramparts. The sudden constraint of time.

A black cat emerged from the shed in the courtyard. It peered at me from the darkness.

The next time I knocked on the door at 12 rue des Juifs, I heard footsteps. The door opened. It was a small boy—perhaps six years old. He looked at me without saying a word. He rubbed his eyes, staring straight ahead, past me.

I asked, Is your mother or father at home?

He didn't respond.

A few moments later, I heard a baby crying in the background. Some shuffling from within the dark corridor. It was a warm afternoon. The lights were off. Perhaps the family had been asleep. Finally, a woman came to the door. She wore a pale blue sundress. She carried a baby in her arms. She said, May I help you?

I said, I'm very sorry. I hope I didn't disturb you.

No, she said. Can I help you?

The baby continued to cry. She hugged it closer to her body.

I said, I'm looking for a Madame Brissac. I believe she lives here. Or has lived here.

Madame Brissac? No, she said. My family has lived here for generations.

I'm sorry to have disturbed you, I said. I must have the wrong address.

She said, Brissac? The name? she asked. Not familiar. Juif? she asked.

Yes, I said. I believe so.

Not possible, she said.

Someone in the village might know, I said.

No, she said. I doubt it. Jews haven't lived in this village for over five hundred years.

I stepped back.

She said, Not here.

I leaned against the water well in the courtyard.

12

Moss grew around and along the stone structure. I sat down on the broken wooden bench next to the well. Birds everywhere. Everywhere their sound. The day increasingly humid. Footsteps in the distance.

The bus arrived outside the upper gate—just beyond the old ghetto. I got on, the doors closing behind me. The bus descended, winding down around the fortressed walls of the village.

It was early spring—the green hillsides covered in grapevines. The heat was stifling. I sat in the middle of the bus—filled with young students and elderly women. No one spoke.

In the valley the bus stopped again—at an isolated stop. No village. Just a bench on the side of the road. A man got on. He sat in the seat across the aisle from me.

He said, Can I open the window for you?

I'm fine, I said. Thank you.

He smiled.

Laughter came from the back of the bus. I turned around. Two young boys wrestled each other in their seats.

My back was wet. I wiped my upper lip. He continued to watch me.

He said, You're visiting?

Yes, I answered.

For long?

Not sure, I answered.

He smiled again. Taking off his dark blue jacket, he folded it across his lap. He turned his body to face mine.

The bus driver shouted at the children. Hey, he yelled, you kids in the back. I turned around. The two boys giggled.

The man said, I'm interested in your face. I'm an artist.

I shook my head, not knowing what to say.

I'd like to photograph you, he said.

I'm not sure, I answered.

He said, Of course, I understand.

I pulled the fabric of the dress away from my body.

We're coming to my stop, he said. He pulled out a pen and small notebook from the pocket of his jacket. He said, I'm setting up an exhibit in this village. I'll write down the address. I think you'll enjoy it. He tore out the page from his notebook, reaching across the aisle to hand the note to me.

I took it from him.

He held out his hand. Luca Corbeau, he said. Please come by.

The bus stopped at the next village. He got off, turning back to look at me. He smiled before he turned to enter through the village gates.

The bus passed two more villages before crossing a bridge over a narrow river and stopping at an industrial outpost. About to exit, I asked the driver for directions to the old cemetery. He shrugged. I wouldn't know, he said.

It was now late afternoon. I walked through two roundabouts. On either side, white block buildings, deserted parking lots. Forgotten, abandoned. At the second roundabout there was a small white sign pointing east: *Cimetiere Juif.* I followed the sign.

Occasionally a car passed, honking at me as I walked along the empty streets. At each crossroad, I stopped. No place to hide. Where could I go? The sun beat down. The heat unbearable. Inside my shoes, my feet swelled.

At the next roundabout, the road ended. The ground grew marshy—wet. To the right—a white path leading up into the hills. To the left, the road, with no sign, appeared to lead back to the village. I crossed a small bridge over the marshy landscape. Weeds and wildflowers grew tall. Cicadas. Birds. No sign of human life. I passed a farm. No workers, no animals.

I followed a narrow dirt path toward and around a high cement wall. Across the way—a small two-story brick structure, perhaps a house, surrounded by a wire fence. Still no movement. Inside the fence—a tractor, barrels, weeds. As I passed, two Rottweilers inside the fence ran at me, barking, sniffing, digging at the dirt at the bottom of the fence. I couldn't breathe. I passed the house, walking on.

The cemetery gates were closed but not locked. I pushed them open and went inside—the ground covered in white gravel. The light reflecting off the whiteness. Inside, a landscape of dark tombstones. Some so blackened it was impossible to read the names.

The cemetery extended in two directions. A small chapel in the back.

I turned to the left side of the cemetery, holding my purse close to my body. The writing on the tombstones worn away, barely decipherable. Only dates. No names. 1896, 1897, 1889, 1888.

Silence broke. A truck drove up the dirt path, stopping at the two-story structure outside the cemetery gates. The dogs barked. A train passed in the woods behind the cemetery.

I stood just inside the cemetery gates waiting— waiting to see what the driver would do. He pulled into the yard next to the house. Two men got out of the truck and began unloading boxes. The dogs ran up to the men. The men didn't notice me. I waited until they left before I moved.

At the entrance to the graveyard stood a large monument to the victims of the Holocaust. I don't know why I proceeded. With each step the gravel beneath my feet cracked—as if at any moment the silence of the landscape would eviscerate me—the stone stelae, crumbling.

Who had gone here before? Who had surrendered? The names on the stones, now—barely discernable. Only dates.

I passed among the unknown with only a marker to show that they had once been here. Where were their families now? Where had they gone? No sign of flowers—of movement—of visitors—to remember them.

As I walked I imagined I was walking with my father—where was my mother's stone—so far away now—across an ocean—across a continent? Not here. But where? Absent of the verdant wasteland between us.

My father and I wandered the cemetery, looking for the names of our family. Of my family's family. He said, I used to know where your grandmother was buried. He said, I don't know where my father is.

I said, It's here. But where?

He said, I need to clean the stones for them. I'm now the gatekeeper.

A mockingbird landed on top of a tombstone, squawking three times before flying off.

The door to the chapel was locked. I turned around,

searching for dates, searching for names. The rows of dead.

I read the names that were visible.
Kahn, Dryfus, Weil.
Marceu. Ackerman. Marx. Levy.
Lieberman. Loeb. Ratisbonne.
See. Strauss.
Cahan, Levy. Levy. Villon.
Wyler, Wyler, Vigee.

At what point did names become things, pointing to a history I no longer understood?

Fischer, Gutman, Klatzki, Braun. The landscape of the inevitable.

At the juncture between the third and fourth row, I saw it—the name Brissac carved into the stone. I touched it—afraid to feel what I feared most—the name on the tombstone: Abraham Brissac. B. 1849. D. 1906. Was it the same? Same Brissac? Same family? Above his name, the carved image of a book.

At first I kneeled, then sat down on the white gravel. The earth was hot—the stones painful. I pulled my notebook out of my purse, pulling a piece of paper from it. I wrote the words: I will find you. I folded the paper and buried it among the warm stones in front of the grave.

At the entrance gate there was a faucet and a basin below it. I turned the spigot. It did not work.

I walked out to the highway. The bus that was supposed to arrive that afternoon didn't come. Though it was still light out, I could see that darkness would arrive soon.

I sat down on the bench. I looked up. Imagining I could see. Stranded here. In a place unfamiliar, resonant with lies—half-truths—sounds that echoed in an open space—surfaced in the closed and claustrophobic world that refused to change.

What action repairs the expanse of breath—a moment and time—breathless beneath the exposure to other.

I followed Luca's note to the next village in the valley. There was a small market in the center of town—just past the central fountain: a vegetable stand, a butcher, a baker selling bread. A woman at a table selling handmade beaded jewelry and trinkets. The morning—already hot, unseasonably warm. The grey cobblestone streets radiated heat. The light—early spring. Pollen in the air—drifting. Flower pots lined the windows of the half-timbered buildings. There were a few shoppers there, older women, carrying bags and rolling carts, speaking to purveyors at the stands.

I wandered through the market and up the hill toward the arched city gates. Most cafes and restaurants were still closed.

I sat down on the edge of the stone fountain in the middle of the square. I took out my notebook. I wrote: I no longer know where I am or where I am going. I cannot find him. I cannot find her. I cannot find. I closed my eyes in the early morning heat.

I contemplated the names of each village—each village I had walked, speaking the names, the sounds. The inability to recreate those sounds to give meaning to those names. Names listed and crossed out. Each rue des Juifs—a forgotten street. A landscape of forgotten names, of forgotten dreams. Of being transformed, remade. Perhaps this—here.

I took out my grandfather's diary. I looked down at the first page: Regimental No. 203th. Rank: Cpl. Name: Gutman. A log of villages.

I passed through each village. Each village he had passed through. I held his diary.

When he came off the train in Dover, the wounded passed him, moving toward the city.

He moving past them. Through them.

April 16, 1918. Tuesday: France. Left Calais for training camps. By train. Hiked to village near firing line. Hiked all day. Could hardly walk.

Had he been here? In this village? Of the ordinary— of the extraordinary.

I held his diary. Kept it close. How could I enter his consciousness? Few words. Days/weeks/months/ names—each village a reminder of the previous village—of the next village—only names. Names recorded. Names checked off. Each village—a semblance of the last. And his entry: Cannot find Brissac.

At the corner of the Grand rue and the rue de la Croix, a sign taped to a light post advertised Luca's art exhibit at 17 rue des Juifs. I stopped a woman rolling a cart on the street and asked her for directions. She looked carefully at the poster. Though it was a small village, at first she seemed as if she had never heard of that place—or didn't quite know how to direct me there. She looked at me, then said, Yes. I know where it is. Her cart was filled with cheeses and dried meats, radishes, lettuces, tomatoes, flowers. She pointed to a small street that led from the square. It's not far, she said.

I entered the narrow street—just past a butcher shop that was now closed. In the window a poster with the words, Chez L'Artisan Boucher. Below that the image of a grazing cow. The windows were closed above the shop. The façade—a weave of brown wooden banding. At the corner, a road sign read: *Sauf Riverains*.

The landscape was absent of movement. The yellow and ochre lime-washed walls—the half-timbered roofs. The cobblestone street—static, removed.

Two elderly women sat in folding chairs in the alley behind the butcher shop, their eyes closed in the afternoon sun. Mid-afternoon sunlight broke against the timber roof, casting deep shadows across the women.

The synagogue was on the other side of the alley. The arched wooden doors were open. Inside, the colors a reflection of the outside world. Yellow—ochre—

white. Cut into the red tile entry, a glass floor. Beneath it a stone cistern.

The light was bright inside the space. Open. Expansive. I walked through the second set of arched wooden doors. On either side—sandstone arcades. Within each arcade an arched window. The walls were painted a soft yellow. The space—light, tile, stone. A grey and white-tiled mosaic covered the back wall.

Luca stood in the far side of the space—to the right of the altar—studying a sculpture. He turned around. He took off his glasses. He hesitated at first, then smiled, tousling his shaggy grey hair. He stepped back—away from the sculpture. What do you think? he asked.

It was a large figure—blue legs, black body, a red beak. The figure—suspended—hovering in the corner of the room.

Light from the circular windows in the upper gallery illuminated the creature, creating an otherworldly haze around it. Its vibrant colors pierced the silence of the space.

An Oiseau, he said. Part of a series. An aviary of sorts.

I walked closer. Half-man-half-bird. The head tilted, the face a beak. Arms in place of wings. The blue tail—a third leg.

We installed him this morning. I've named him Big Bird. Funny?

I tried to smile.

He took a step toward me. The others are still in the studio, he said. We open next week. He fiddled with his glasses, tossing them from one hand to the other.

I couldn't discern Luca's age. At once young—the way he dressed, the way he moved. And yet, there was something in him that betrayed that youth. Something in his eyes. Distant, reflective. As though he were judging me. Studying me.

You should come to my studio, he said. The space is smaller, of course. Less intimidating. He gestured as though he were about to speak—then stopped.

Yes, I said. I would like to.

Are you here for long? he asked.

I don't know.

He turned to face the sculpture. You know, my birds, my creatures, he said, I'm just one in a long history of artists trying to find the body that can exhibit the quest.

What do you mean? I asked.

He laughed. Oh, he said. What is the body, after all—life, death—the expectation of significance? That ambiguous relationship between the natural world, the spiritual world, the world of fantasy. He spoke, moving his arms in the air as if to illustrate an impossible point. Then he became quiet.

What is the quest?

He laughed.

I stepped closer. Unable to articulate what I felt, what I thought.

What is it? I asked.

He thought for a minute. An echo of reality, he said. He looked down. The desire for imagination? To understand the body? Don't all artists do that?

Do they?

You? he asked. What do you think?

I shuddered. The creature—fancifully grotesque. A gargoyle, a griffin. Here. In this place. I couldn't imagine the space—filled with these creatures—neither human nor animal—in the liminal world between.

No need to say anything, he said. An unfair question. He took a step toward me. Touch the piece, he said. Don't be afraid.

I came closer.

Please, he said.

I put my hand out. He took it, placing it on the figure's beak. The surface of the sculpture was cold. The texture rough. Up close—the feathers were eyes. A series of red eyes with black corneas—an elaborate construction.

I'm glad you came, he said. I thought you might.

I pulled my hand back.

Art shouldn't be seen from a distance, he said. Should it? I want my art integrated into the viewer's life. I want the viewer to see himself as a part of my art. I don't think of myself as an artist. I call myself a poet.

I didn't answer.

And you? he asked.

I said, I'm a writer. I'm not sure why I said that. It seemed foreign—out of place. Untrue.

I thought so, he smiled. He pointed to the circular stained glass window upstairs, the image—petals of a flower. Go up there, he said. Where you see the oculus—a rose window. There's a narrow passageway at the entrance. Be careful.

I looked back at him.

I want to know about your writing, he said.

I took the narrow winding stairs to the second floor. The steps were shallow. I held on to the worn wooden banister. At the top, a second level—a gallery of worship for the women. Wood benches lined the perimeter. The benches didn't face inward toward the altar, rather they faced outward—toward small round windows cut into the yellow-washed walls. I looked down toward the altar—the height made me lightheaded. I thought about my mother. Then. Now. In that moment. The last image I had of her. Her eyes closed. Her body—frail, still—in her coffin.

The stained glass window cast a swirling image of red and yellow on the wood plank floor.

When was this synagogue built? I asked.

Originally medieval, Luca said. I believe there was a fire. It was rebuilt in the 19th century. He pointed to the back wall, above the altar. You see that mosaic on the wall—it's Roman. Remarkable, isn't it? They discovered it when a builder tore down a house next door. What's left of a villa. He looked down. He said, It must all be here—that city—below our feet.

And now? This space?

For exhibitions and concerts. Beautiful, isn't it? Clean lines—linear. Not what you'd expect from a synagogue.

I said, Does anyone come here?

What do you mean? he asked.

To pray, I said.

I wouldn't know, he said. I'm not from here. But this isn't a space for prayer, he said. Not now.

Yes, I said. I had heard that there was one family left here—the Brissacs?

Who? he asked.

I'm trying to find Madame Brissac.

I can check for you, he said. I'll ask the locals.

We stood in silence—the Oiseau floating in the corner.

He said, I hope you'll come back.

Yes, I said. I will.

Where are you staying? he asked.

I have a room in a neighboring village.

I'm staying here in a studio near the Hotel Colombier, he said. Just for the exhibition. The hotel is simple but clean, and interesting. It's quiet this week. I'm sure they'll have a room for the night. And dinner? he asked.

I returned to the previous village and collected my luggage.

I checked into the Colombier—on the banks of a small canal that wove through the center of the village. The one room left was at the top of a narrow wooden stairway. The hotel clerk told me that it was an upgrade. They had just finished remodeling it. 15th century, she said. She handed me the key. She said, I think you will be pleased.

The room was spare, clean and modern. I entered through the red door. Inside, a bed, a nightstand, a writing desk. A small white-tiled bathroom. The room was emptied of objects. Only those things that referred to nothing. No sense of here. Of anywhere. A pencil. A small notepad placed next to the telephone. Inside the closet—three hangers and a bag for laundry.

The window looked out over the courtyard of the hotel. In the corner a white stone sculpture of a wine jug rose above the roofline of the courtyard. I put down my bag and took off my watch, placing it on the nightstand. I noted the time. 4:00 p.m.

I woke to voices outside my window. Laughter. Screams. More laughter. Footsteps. I thought I heard children.

I pulled back the gauze curtain. Opened the window. Below in the hotel courtyard a couple sat drinking white wine, speaking softly. A family sat with a small child. The hotel clerk brought out a tea setting on a platter. She placed the porcelain teacups in front of the family. She handed the child a cup and poured him tea.

The sky darkened above the narrow courtyard. The air felt damp. It grew increasingly heavy. A dank smell rose from the green canal water. I shut the window.

I opened the half-bottle of red wine in the mini-bar. I poured myself a glass. I took a sip. Curling up on the bed, I closed my eyes.

Image slipped into memory. Erased. Consciousness. Bled into the fine corners of space.

I had the sense that someone was beside me.

He got out of bed. What a nightmare, he said.

I said, What happened?

He said, I don't want to tell you.

Please, I asked.

He went to the bathroom. He came back.

I said, What was it?

The gas chambers, he said. So real, he said. The

vision so real. Present, here. He left the room. From the doorway, he said, I need to be alone. I need to think. Wish me luck. He said, Wish me luck.

Perhaps an hour had passed, perhaps two. When I looked out the window again, the grass seemed greener than before. Was that real? I held the window open. The rain had begun. Slowly, softly, increasing and persistent. The sky heavy and grey. Footsteps across the gravel. It seemed that hours had passed—even days. I could not be certain of time. Had I entered a waking dream world? So distant—so within reach.

From my window I could see across the grass and stone courtyard to the rooms on the other side. The curtains were open in the room across from me. Through the window—the faint outline of a man and a woman. He, in a chair, holding a book. She, standing before a mirror. He put his book down on the nightstand next to a water glass and went over to her. She stood motionless for a moment before turning around to face him. Their movements as unreal as the green of the grass. And yet, as ordinary. Still and stable. Slow—articulated. Their presence there—a part of the landscape. She turned from him, walking across the room and over to the window, opening it. She looked out across the courtyard. She put her hand out—into the air—perhaps testing it for temperature. I could not see her features—but could feel them. I pulled back from the window. She stood there for a moment—looking out again in my direction before closing the window and drawing the curtains.

The air felt cool—the dampness of the green world penetrating the room. The gravel blackened by water. The courtyard empty now—a few tables and the tea setting that had been left.

What prevented my movement. Any movement too fragile for the range of decision. The book on the table. The bell captain walking across the stone courtyard, wearing a dark hat.

Each sound—each vision—fractured by the wordless persistence of the image I could not evade. I wanted to sit and read a book. I wanted to stand before the mirror. I wanted to be the couple in the room. When I looked out again, I saw the bell captain walk across the courtyard in the persistent, dampening rain.

I lost track of time. I could not stay here alone in this room. In this moment. I grew impatient. I put on my watch. I took out my black dress from my bag, unfolding it on the bed, smoothing out the lines that had formed.

I stood in front of the bathroom mirror. I took out my makeup case. I re-applied my black eyeliner and then my red lipstick. In the bathroom light, my face looked garish. Each mark accentuated. My skin aging.

The creases around my eyes, around my mouth, formed. Too late. Too late. I stood back. Perhaps in the dimmed light of the hotel restaurant, he would not notice. I wiped off the lipstick. I thought about my mother. The lines around my mouth were stained pink. I saw her image in me. My image—absent. I washed my face again. I re-applied the lipstick.

The bar downstairs in the hotel lobby looked out at the central courtyard. The rain had stopped. Three guests sat at a wrought iron table next to the sculpture of the wine jug. The young woman leaned against the man sitting next to her. Across from the couple—an older man held a camera, occasionally picking it up to look through the viewfinder. The couple laughed, holding their glasses. The older man took pictures of them.

Early evening spring light reflected off the stucco walls in the courtyard. Each wall painted a different color—blue, white, burnt orange. The woman's shadow, linked with the man's, cast an amorphous fluid shape on the white stone wall behind them.

I ordered a gin and tonic.

Will you be joining us for dinner? the bartender asked.

I'm waiting for someone, I said.

Sure, he answered. He brought back a tall glass with gin and opened a bottle of tonic water.

I took out my grandfather's diary. The map of the ship. The bow, the stern. Each level. Each space. Marked, numbered. Represented by the sequence of movement—movement toward the unknown. Trying to make sense of it. Setting off across the ocean. From Halifax. A full moon. He, writing: Somewhere on the sea.

I noted the time in my notebook—half-past 7:00. I wrote down the name Brissac. Circled it, then unfolded a small map of the countryside. I listed the villages in the valley that I had been to. Below that I drew a map of the landscape. Each village connected to the next by long suspension bridges.

The gin calmed me a bit. As though I were floating in a slow-moving stream—movement barely discernable.

I looked down toward the end of the bar. A woman sat, sipping a glass of white wine. She reminded me of my neighbor who had come by the day before I left. She had come to the door, holding a glass of wine. And a white flower she had just picked from her garden. How long will you be gone? she asked.

I couldn't tell her. I said, I'm not sure.

You'll keep in touch, I hope. Don't worry, she said. We'll watch the place while you're gone.

How long has it been? The image recedes. Quietly. Reappearing without warning. Moments of being.

With what seemed at once unexpected, and at once completely natural, a sudden storm. The rain poured down—flashes of lightening. The world gave way. The sense that space is no longer ours—the doors to the courtyard opened and the photographer and the couple ran in, laughing, drenched, shaking off the water with delight. They ran to a table behind me. They sat down, laughing. Giddy. The room spun with laughter.

The photographer came up to the bar next to me. He looked at me, laughing. Where to next? he asked. He put his camera down on the bar and ordered three beers. Through for the day? he asked.

I guess so, I said.

Italian? he asked. Russian?

No, I said.

Not American, he said. I don't think so.

I said, Yes. I am.

Your family? Not American. I'm sure of it.

He picked up two of the beers, took them to the couple at the table. They exchanged a few words. He came back to the bar. Jew, he said. He pointed to my face. I can always tell faces, he said. That's my job.

He lifted his camera from the bar, slung it over his shoulder. He picked up the third beer and gestured to me. Cheers, he said and returned to his table.

From the far side of the bar, the woman lifted her glass, raised it, taking a final sip. She signed her bill. She came over to me.

She said, I'm here on business. She reached into her purse, pulled out a card and handed it to me. I sell pottery made on my island. They like it here. The bright colors. The primitive designs. It appeals to a certain Northern sensibility. They come to our island every spring. It's a volcanic island. A dry climate. The mineral waters. They want light. I come twice a year and stay in this hotel. It's a bit cold here—but comfortable and clean. How long are you here for? she asked.

Not sure, I said. I don't have any plans to return home. Not yet. I twisted my mother's ring, her grandmother's ring, which I wore on my index finger. It was too big. I often checked to make sure it was still there. She noticed.

She said, I have a meeting to go to at a tourist shop in the center of town. You have my card, she said. I leave tomorrow. If you need anything, she pointed to the card. Please come to my island, she said. It's beautiful. The landscape, the food. When you come, please call me. I'll show you around. She said, I can see you're a person who has lived a life filled with an almost painful awareness of what it means to live. She put her hand on top of mine.

I flinched. She didn't remove her hand.

She leaned in closer to me. I felt her breath. The sweet scent of perfume that lingered on her clothing.

When you come, please call me. You'll love the food, the wine, the fish.

She lifted her hand off mine.

While you're here, she said, be careful. Don't tell anyone where your family is originally from. She walked away.

I picked up the card she had left me. Her name, Iris Bloch. On the back—a phone number and address, written in pencil.

A short while later, Luca arrived. He put his hand on my shoulder. I hope I haven't kept you waiting. He said, Let's get out of here—go somewhere else. It's too formal here, don't you think? He stopped, paused. Then said, I just heard about a concert tonight—in the cathedral.

We walked up the street and then up a series of stairs to a church located on the highest point in the village, on a hill that looked out over the vine-covered countryside, the castle in the hazy distance.

The sign on the light post out front read: *Mendelssohn: Piano Concerto No. 1. Schubert: Symphony No. 9, "The Great".*

He said, You're out of breath?

I'm fine, I said.

Are you sure? he asked.

The wooden doors to the church were open. He said, What do you think? Shall we?

An usher at the door handed me a program. She held two fingers up to her lips, cautioning us to be quiet. The orchestra is about to begin, she said. She pointed toward a pew in the back.

We sat down. A woman sitting next to me leaned over and whispered in my ear, Perfect seats. Just the right distance from the music.

The conductor entered the stage. He faced the

audience, bowed. Laughed. Then turned toward the orchestra.

From the far left, a woman in a red gown followed, bowed, then sat down at the piano.

The audience applauded. Luca put his hand on top of mine.

On the brink of silence. The orchestra's brief exuberant beginning. The pianist entering the music—in flight—delicate, powerful, redolent with the expression of life. Luca pulled his hand away from mine.

Forget, I thought. As the music begins. The scales, the chords. The orchestra again. Each urgency a moment in the way in which we sat here together. The rapid and prolonged passage into the watery unknown. The space around us—the music filling that open space, the vaulted ceiling, the stained glass windows. The stillness of the room. The keys weaving in and out in their rupture with the present. Intricate, fleeting. The figures woven into the fabric of the countryside. The landscape the question. The hills, the villages, the past. The sounds unlimited in their attention to the delicate and powerful conflict. The range in which the music responded to the beauty—into the unbroken quality of the need to expect.

I looked at Luca. His eyes were closed. The woman next to me sat forward on the edge of her seat.

The audience silent—still.

A crucifix hung over the altar.

The orchestra once again began its thematic reprisal in dialogue with the pianist. The piano changed tone. The conductor lost in the reverie of dream—sounds at once together and at odds. The lyrical slowing of time and space.

Each space a contemplation of the illusory night. A night—the music—captured in the romantic reverie of story. Luca's closed eyes. My inability to understand who he was in that moment. The outside chance that we would sit here together in this space where music advanced through repetition, the theme developing its dialogue—searching amidst the space of desire. The calm break in the night—an expression of the absence of calm. I looked back at Luca. His eyes closed. Distant.

The rapid acceleration of the pianist's hands moving across the keys. Ascending. Descending. Leaping octaves. Of night, of spring, of the anticipation of summer. Of the countryside that succumbed to the background accompaniment of the woodwinds, strings, brass. Woven through and into the foreign space. Of this moment here and now that I would not remember—that I would need to forget.

Silence and fire. Beauty and nothingness now returned. The background. Mysterious—yet—brutally familiar. Where I was. Where I entered into this space and sound. Luca, the man who sat next to me with his eyes closed. The woman who sat next to me on the edge of her seat. The audience immobile. Lost in the moment in the inexplicable silence broken by the wordless movement of fire. The pianist on the edge of her piano bench. The crucifix hanging above the altar. The altar where the musicians played. The stained glass images, stories of creation and destruction, surrounding the space that encapsulated the space. The slowing of— then rapid ascent into the mystery. On this hillside in this town. Absent the answer. Alluding to the dialogue, the flurry of flight moving into melancholy—always unattainable.

I found my hands clenched. Numb. The beauty of the music. The trancelike softness that countered the power of the orchestra's relentless attempt to bring the music out of lostness into urgency.

Luca opened his eyes. Turned toward me. Looked down at my clenched hands. Smiled. Then returned to face the orchestra, closing his eyes once again. The pianist's rapid elaborate finger work, replacing the slowing reverie of the evening dream. Dreamlike acceptance of the unknown.

The audience sat for a moment as one in the soaring space we sat in together.

We did not stay for the Schubert. It might have invaded that space in the body and the mind where the Mendelssohn resonated.

Luca led me a short distance down the cobblestone street. He walked fast, with determination, turning to look back at me, making sure—it seemed—that I was still behind him. Each time he looked back at me, he smiled. We did not talk. The music followed us. The music became us. Without any need to speak. We moved through the village—at first in elation—then found ourselves caught in the need to escape the reverie that had set in upon us.

At one point Luca stopped in front of a shop window. We both stopped. He pointed to our reflections in the glass superimposed upon the trinkets in the shop. Small figurines of men and women. Elfin creatures. Creatures with exaggerated faces—expressions of wild pleasure—of uncertain pain. Painted red cheeks. White teeth. There were storks, witches, toy wooden houses. He put his arm around my waist as though posing for a photograph. Strange, isn't it? Beautiful. Grotesque. The image of village life. How can I capture that? he asked. Somewhat naïve? he asked. Primitive? The essence of superstition? He pulled me closer to him. He turned to me. What do you think? He didn't wait for my answer. Ok. Enough of that for now. We'll get back to that later.

He took his arm from my waist, taking my hand. Come on, he said.

He led me a short distance down the cobblestone street to a tavern next to the river. Onward, to dine, he said.

The red-canopied restaurant patio next to the river was filled, noisy. There were families, tourists. Perhaps a few locals. A blur of bodies. Of sound. We went inside.

It was a small dark room, angular, tight. Candles lit on every table. The room glowed. A woman at the desk greeted Luca, picked up two menus, then led us to a secluded table near the kitchen.

You see, he said. Much better. He leaned back in his chair. Cocked his head. Looked at me. Smiled. He looked over to the waitress at the next table, motioning for her to bring us some wine. The end of a long but rewarding day, he said.

The usual? she asked.

She came back with two glasses and a carafe of white wine. She set the glasses down on the red-checkered oilcloth, then poured us each a glass.

He said, This place is one of my favorites. Regional cooking. Rustic. It's been here for decades. Always dependable. Are you familiar with the food around here? He lifted his glass. He said, To a fortunate meeting.

I lifted my glass. Yes. And to a wonderful concert, I said.

I took a sip. The wine tasted of minerals, of earth. Yet a certain sweetness emerged from it.

They're known for their whites around here, he said. If you prefer, we'll switch to red when the food comes.

He set his glass down, leaned across the table. What did you think about the concert? he asked.

I can't stop thinking about it, I said. The energy. The room. I don't think I've heard Mendelssohn in that way before. Experienced that before. Live. In concert. Moving us from ecstasy to dream.

Yes, he said. Moving. Palpable. The room alive.

I don't know much about him. About Mendelssohn.

An interesting story, he said. His biography. His family history.

I need to know more, I said. About him. His work.

Yes, he said. We'll talk more. For now, you need to tell me about your work. What you do. Why you're here.

My face grew warm. I didn't know what to say. I hoped he wouldn't press me. I couldn't stop thinking about the music. I heard it and, yet, I couldn't hear it. I sat back. Took another sip of wine. When I looked up, I noticed a black bowler hat hanging from the ceiling—above the table. Used as a fixture. A single bare bulb hung from within. There were bowler hats everywhere—over most of the tables—three in the corner of the room—hanging from thin black wires. The dark hats perverted the light, casting amorphous shadows in the room. Darkness penetrated the corners. A man sat alone at the next table with a plate of meat. He ate slowly, meticulously.

Luca followed my eyes. Funny, isn't it? he said. Devilishly fun.

What is it?

He raised his hands in a gesture above his head. A bit of whimsy, he said. Surrealism. Perhaps a reference to Chaplin—or Magritte. Or even Beckett.

Strange, I said. To dine under a bowler hat.

I looked up to the ceiling. The bare lightbulb hanging within the hat. The light momentarily blinding me.

He said, Yes. But the image is multifaceted—impossible to reduce. The modern man. The banker. Once the image of the businessman. The Nazis outlawed it—called it Judenstahlhelm. Used it in anti-Semitic cartoons.

The waitress came over. She said, It's white asparagus season. She pointed to the hand-written menu on the wall. She suggested the white asparagus terrine with morels. A specialty of the house.

Let's start there, he said. I hope you don't mind. He turned to me. Such a short season, he said. The original chef's been gone for a number of years—but the new chef keeps up the traditions.

I couldn't shake the strange feeling of dining under a hat. I thought of my mother's collection of hats—of the hats I never saw her wear. Still in a box in the corner of her closet. Of the image of my grandfather in the war—in his uniform—wearing his doughboy hat—on leave with three other soldiers. His peculiar, enigmatic smile—neither happy nor sad—looking straight into the camera. Of how hats needed to be removed in a restaurant and here we were dining beneath them. The three hats in the corner.

Luca said, Is everything okay? You look distracted.

The room grew increasingly close. Warm. The image of the man—straddling the old and new world. Where was he and why was this hat all that remained? The businessman. Disembodied. Removed. A fragment of the original. The ridiculed Jew in Nazi propaganda.

I picked up my fork, turning it in my hand.

Luca said, Perhaps you don't like it here?

No, I answered. I do.

He watched me playing with my fork. I put it down. Unfolded my napkin. Took another sip of wine. I wondered about the sophisticated women he usually had dinner with. I suddenly felt too young, too naive. An absurd thought, I told myself. One look in the mirror.

He poured me another glass. I looked over at the man at the next table, eating meat and cabbage, drinking wine. The heat in the restaurant overwhelming.

I asked him what brought him here—for the exhibit.

46

Such a small town. Was there a large art community here?

He told me that you can't separate the region and art. Just look at the concert tonight. Unexpected. It's embedded in the culture. Even in the smallest village. In any case, his exhibit is not hard to reach from any city center. His assistant, Inès, had arranged it. She's from here. Luca fell in love with the space. Soaring ceilings—wonderful light. He said, My studio isn't far from the space. I hope you'll visit. I'll be in town for the month. This, for instance. He pointed to the light fixture above us. Not conventional—unexpected. It makes you think, doesn't it?

Yes, I said. It seems violent.

Is it? he asked. If so, is that a bad thing? he asked. Isn't violence energy?

I didn't respond. My endeavor here—unclear. Undefined.

Luca noticed my discomfort. He said, Take Christian art. The medieval artist. Christ's suffering body. The martyrdom of the saints. The depiction of hell. Isn't it all blood-soaked? He said, This medieval landscape. This building, he said. What happened here—or in the river this building sits on the banks of.

I said, I couldn't imagine. I made lists in my mind. The shuttered windows. The cobblestone streets. The murky water in the river, in the canals.

You need to see the Isenheim Altarpiece. We can go together, he suggested.

I said, Yes. I've wanted to see it. I planned on it. Researched it.

He said, Part of your work?

I didn't know how to answer him. I said, I think that you can't understand this place without seeing it. That it's tied to the history of what's happened here.

In what sense? he asked.

I'm not sure. I fumbled. I'm sorry, I said. I don't know what I'm trying to say.

He said, One of the greatest works of all time—also one of the most gruesome. Painted to heal the sick. To give solace. Christ's battered body. The devil's taunting in the background.

He stopped. Grew silent. Thoughtful. Sat back. Well, he said, when the food comes, we should eat. He laughed.

The server returned. Madame, Monsieur, I hope everything is all right. The server placed the terrines in front of us.

I think you'll enjoy this, he said.

I took a bite. The white asparagus—creamy, custard-like. It was a struggle to eat. Each bite difficult to swallow. Too rich. In this heat, especially. And yet, I wanted to feel the landscape, understand the food. What the Brissacs had eaten, if they had dined here.

You know, he said, when my father told me stories of being a prisoner of war—he didn't recollect those times with dread—even though they were certainly dreadful. But he was young. And in his youth—it seemed as though the moments were vivid. Exceptional. I think for him—he was, oddly, alive. Energy in the depths of destruction—despair. All experience, he said. Even this. Can we hide from violence?

When the waitress returned, she suggested the pork knuckles with potato salad.

You'll enjoy them, he said.

She left. The room suddenly grew quiet. Guests had begun to leave.

So, now, he said, and you? You haven't answered me. Please tell me what you're working on.

I made up a story—a half-truth. I said, I'm working on a book about my grandfather. He fought near here—in the First World War. I have his diary, I said. I'm following his steps. The places he'd been to. Trying to understand him. He never spoke about the war—according to my father. And, I never really knew him. I just have fragments, pieces. Of a life. Of his life. But much of it is erased. So it's strange that you brought up your father. His experience during the war.

This is a kind of connection, he said. Serendipity. Perhaps, even fate.

I took the diary out of my purse. I kept it in a small envelope.

Luca reached across the table. He took the envelope, took out the diary. He turned it over. Opened it to the first page. To his regiment. His name: Joseph Gutman. His home address. Corps. Company. Platoon. The date: September 29th 1917.

The pages were fragile—I feared they would disintegrate. The words barely legible.

It's beautiful, he said. A treasure.

I agreed. Then said, But it's not beautiful. I can't see this book—this experience as beautiful. Filled with violence. Fear. The unknown.

But this diary itself, he said. It's precious.

Yes.

He said, Your grandfather—my father—they fought the same war. WWI became WWII became...?

I've tried to reconcile this—that war he fought in— the world he fought for—with this, here, now.

He continued to turn the pages. Noting the images. Points on a compass. Finding your direction by day. Finding your direction by night. Conventional signs and lettering used in military field sketching. A guide to life, he said.

I'm afraid to hold it, I said. But I don't have a choice.

He said, I can see this is very important for you. You've been following him?

I'm not sure why. Why I'm so drawn to this journal?

Of this man I never knew. Of this place? Of this landscape?

You're writing a fiction?

Yes, I answered. At least, I believe so. It's up to me to write his story. I don't want to take liberties with his story, with his life. What choice do I have? It's difficult to imagine—what he went through. What he saw. The women he writes about—the woman he left behind when he went to war.

He said, I'd love to be a part of this project. I'd love to help you. Inès arrives tomorrow. She knows this place. She knows the people.

That would be helpful, I said.

He handed me back the diary. He said, We need to go together to see the Altarpiece. You need to see this—to understand this place. As important as the food.

The waitress arrived with our dinner. She set the plates before us.

I said, I don't know this dish.

Then you're in for a treat. A signature dish of the region.

The meat was moist but fatty. Again, as with the first course, each bite was difficult to swallow. I didn't want to let on about my discomfort. Luca ate slowly, meticulously, the way the man at the next table ate. I wasn't sure what I was in for. What I had begun. Why I had begun it. In a strange place, with a man I didn't know. At some point during the meal, Luca said, And the woman—the woman you asked me about? I imagine she is connected.

Madame Brissac. I believe so, I answered.

We'll talk to Inès tomorrow.

I was exhausted. I felt sick. I told him I had to use the restroom.

It's upstairs, he pointed.

I took the winding staircase. At the top there was a small bathroom. A white toilet. A white sink. I looked at myself in the mirror. My features were deformed. Strange. Blurry. My eyes—bloodshot. The heavy pork burned my stomach, my throat.

I thought about the diary, my grandfather's words: On the danger zone. The sea was high & stormy. Met the submarine destroyers. 6 of them. Was on guard today again. Guards placed all around the ship with rifles to watch for submarines. I felt pretty rotten….headache. Today was the experience of my life. Torpedo hit the King Alfred. Was meant for our ship. Carmania. The stern only damaged.

I couldn't stop myself. I leaned over the toilet. I threw up everything that I had.

I woke up in the middle of the night. Under the sheets. Sweating. Much seemed blurry. Our conversations. The night. How I had arrived back at the hotel. I touched my eyes. I was still wearing make-up. The mascara was sticky. I checked the nightstand. The diary was still there. Next to my watch.

What happened last night? Accidents and meanderings led me to the point of refusal.

In this room. In the dark. The night filtered images—faint—phosphorescent. The dark rejected blackness—something absolute. I needed to piece together moments—perhaps hours. All thoughts had disappeared. The dark light played tricks. My eyes did not focus. It was not so much a question of what I could see—but what I could not.

What happened—what I'd forgotten, what I had lost as I experienced it—a question I could not escape.

The question followed me. In bed. Beneath the sheets, beneath the rough blanket. The sounds drifted through me throughout the night. Doors slammed shut. Laughter in the hallway. Women who sounded like girls.

With what had been forgotten came the sense that what I'd lost couldn't be replaced. For I couldn't remember what I felt. You are not cleansed of the past rather you are compelled by the empty street. Feeling is anesthetized. If you forget yourself, you forget all that reminds you of the distance between the language and the moment of desire that ceases the moment you speak. The memories that elude you will disappear. And what replaces them?

The room felt dark. Obscured by darkness. The inconceivable sense that life would have been lived without feeling, without experience. The room existed. It had to exist. I became aware of each molecule in my body. And the sense that I had not been aware of each molecule in my body. How could I forget?

I asked myself to ignore the sounds that penetrated the space which surrounded me. But the collision of memory and the weight of its absence left me without defense. I pulled the blanket over my shoulders over my chin. Lights flickered. Radiating—rhythmic. Reminding me of the persistence of time which prevented the present.

When you forget, do you enter the past or the present? Do you leave behind you the memory of existence?

When I closed my eyes again, I saw a woman drink from the river. She held her hands cupped together. The river flowed from the mountaintop to a juncture—a small break where the water rippled. The icy sting reddened her skin.

The next morning I was walking down the street when Luca joined me. It was a small village, and I imagined that wherever I went, he would find me. We had met earlier in the day at the café next to the hotel. He wanted to take me to see the Altarpiece. A short bus ride, he said. Luca took me down a side street toward the river. We passed timber houses lined with flower-pots and ivy wreaths. Carved wooden figures adorned the facades.

He said, Will you dine with us tonight?

We walked past a shop window displaying leather goods. I stopped. He followed.

The village has a history of the craft of leather making, he said. He pointed to a jacket in the window.

I turned away, our reflections cast in the window. In the water of the river behind us.

Putting his hand on my shoulder, he said, Beautiful, isn't it? One of the few villages saved during the war. Inès loves it here. A sentimental attachment. She asked about you. She hoped she might meet you this evening.

We followed the path through the village. Luca spoke about an oval disk he'd seen in a gallery—made of clay—broken in half. On it were the words of what appeared to be a poem—he couldn't quite recall—the language similar to Latin—a Latin alphabet—and the words faintly familiar—the sounds—familiar—but he couldn't place them. Though he didn't understand that language—the poem left an impression.

He spoke about the food of the region. The specialty bakeries. And the dinner we would have tonight.

The light was bright in the crisp air. Shoppers filled the streets.

How did our words articulate the space around us? The boundaries of presence—of what is seen—of what is not. Place as the coherence of being. Where we are—where we could be. The sense that the space we inhabit is only part of the experience. Had Madame Brissac walked this path? Most likely she had. She must have. Slowly, the day filled the fullness of night. The movement toward evening was the recognition of sounds—blatant in the view of morning.

You can't remember everything. As the mistake of time regenerates the touch of your hand. The register changes key as the movement toward landlocked water. Canals which sound the flow of water.

My grandfather—he'd left obscure notes in his diary. The name Brissac written in the margin. Followed by the words: Can't Find Him. Marching. Hiking. Wearing his gas mask. His handwriting—progressively more difficult to read. The words falling off the page.

Red banners and bright flags strung from the buildings and light posts invigorated the streets with color, reflecting the movement of the river. Feast day. The colors of spring. Yellow. Green. Bridged tone, fusing into summer.

We found ourselves drifting, unaware of the world around us. In the moment. Yellow color absent of sound. Soundless. We hadn't noticed the square filling with strollers and shoppers and groups of cyclists. Their forward momentum. Chaos that enabled the day to begin.

Did he know something about last night? Details, perhaps? About that which I'd lost—that which I couldn't remember. Where I'd gone, where I had been. He seemed to hold something back, to know something that he didn't want to reveal. I felt it in his presence in the way he smiled, as though he held the secret that would bind me to him.

I told him that, in any case, I had already planned to spend the day at the museum, to see the Altarpiece.

He said he could accompany me there. Inès would arrive in the afternoon.

I wanted him to leave my side. For he wouldn't reveal what happened—even as I was certain he knew. The uncertain look on his face. The certainty with which he described the surroundings. The way he led me down the street—walking, turned half toward me, anxious to hold me near him. He asked me to come to his studio.

To see his birds—his sculptures. He persisted. He continued to talk about the village, its traditions, the rituals of the day. How he would show me the woods outside the village. The streams we could hike along. The wildflowers in full bloom.

It occurred to me that he could not leave my side. That what I could not remember held power over him.

Feast day brings us out, he said. It's a religious village. He pulled me to a bakery—toward the sweet yeasty smell. Two, he motioned to the case.

These are the specialty here. He handed me a pastry. Inès's mother used to bake these for her when she was a child. It's an odd Altarpiece, he said. You'll be shocked by its beauty and its horror. Painted to heal the sick.

Groups of children rode past us. Laughing, ringing bells, wearing yellow shirts and red scarves.

He said, Do you remember when we were young? When we did those things?

He spoke about his life—his childhood, reminiscing about weekends in the country, rides in the park. How he had met Inès at the University. The more he spoke, the less I seemed to know him. Words further concealed his being. His intentions obscured. Endless chatter—that couldn't be broken.

When cries broke our isolation, we had to consider how we had abandoned ourselves to the motives that overwhelmed us. Had we heard the crying? We couldn't integrate those sounds into the sounds we desired to hear. We ignored them, I believe. We continued to walk and talk until at some point the crying which grew stronger finally distracted us. We both turned back— only to see a father and son riding together on a bicycle. The son crying. The father pedaling.

We ran to them. The father stopped. His child's foot had become caught in the spokes of the bicycle wheel.

Frozen to what was happening, the father looked behind him, seeing the child scream, blood bleeding through the sock on his son's twisted foot.

Luca said to the father, The boy's hurt. He's hurt badly.

Constraint of images. Wordless. The vase on the table. The old woman in the square. The father and son on the bicycle. The boy in a seat behind the father. The boy screaming. The father focused on sounds beyond, on the forward movement. Why had he failed to hear his son? Forgetting his place. Waves of light that generated blue and red.

What led me to this place? This village? Accident or dilemma? A crack in the earth. Plucked on a string. Each moment braced for danger and the earshot sound of music that I watched in the concert hall. Sitting there, I saw the fingers pluck the sound that broke in the earth below me. And I thought that the music is the dilemma. That earth covered in vast stretches of water sounds blurry—indistinguishable from those sounds meant to be clear. That water that flowed through the city streets.

Why did I stop here? The city now flooded with water. The concert a memory. Was I there last night? Or did I imagine it? Did I watch as the conductor entered the stage, knocking on the door, then laughing at his arrival? The string broke. The violinist tore the loose end. Did I sit next to the woman who painted her eyes and lips and told me that you need to have some distance from the music, or you can't see or hear?

Dampness permeated the village. It lingered. Canals risked the image of symbolism. Fraught with meaning rife with dilemma.

And if I knew what happened, then what? Could I understand the Schubert after the Mendelssohn? Could I follow the ruts in the street, imagine the carriages. The Jews taken to the city gates. The dilemma of being here. The concert hall as a venue for dilemma. The question of the music. The silence that followed the crack in the music when the water covered the city streets, flooding the shops and houses and the belongings that would be thrown out beyond the city gates.

Could I change things? If I could know what it had really meant to be there—here—in this village square— as it had happened? That knowing an impossibility—

the sallow persistence of the dream that faded as I attempted to revive it.

Why did I dream that after the quake we felt the end of the world? That I sat by the phone and, as each caller asked me for help, I shouted back at them without using words. Do I need to know this: why my grandfather returned here? Do I need to know why I dream in words but can't speak them? That when I speak I can't dream. That I can't remember—dates, birthdays, phone numbers, history, names of flowers and trees, birds and insects, the stages of man, the stages of dinosaurs, animal breeds and dictators, poems and people, the difference between gems and minerals, conquering nations, shifting borders, ancient temples, the wonders of the world, constellations, city streets, the teachings of the Vilna Gaon, the music of Schubert and Mendelssohn. If you brought me here to find the history of my people—if I searched for them in this village along these canals, if I looked for them on these cobblestone streets, I would search for them without remembering their names. I would wander this village, this countryside, this landscape. How could I find them? Taken from their homes, vanished. Burned beyond the city gates.

The image persisted. The child's foot. Crushed by the spokes of the wheel.

The boy will be fine, Luca said. He had spoken to the medic.

Under the low grey sky the policeman directed traffic at the village's largest intersection. Not having noticed the clouds. White pollen. Dampness. A sudden spring storm. This happened often, he said. We stood on the corner, not knowing where to turn.

A tall man in a hunter's jacket stopped in front of me, interrupting us. He said, Are you a clown or an actor?

I didn't answer.

It's a tough question, isn't it? he said, before he turned around, then walked away, moving down the street, disappearing into the crowd.

My face grew warm. Conscious of Luca's stare, I looked over. He laughed uncontrollably. His laughter accentuated by his closed eyes, the high cackles that tore through the quiet, the tears that ran down his face—his face that grew red with laughter. He couldn't speak.

We took the local bus from the village gates, traveling through hillsides covered in vineyards, passing broken castle towns, signs that signaled tourist stops, war sites, cemeteries.

We arrived at the museum by late morning. The heat had returned. Crowds flooded the streets, standing in line at the entrance.

Once past the gates, inside the cloister, the crowds dispersed. The space—light and stone—the condition of quiet.

Will I remember this passage under the linden trees—through the stone arcade—surrounding the green courtyard? I will remember this passage—because I must remember something. Behind me the vision of cherry trees. The gravel path. Yellow fields of narcissus. The river that divided the village I had tried to find. Those images that led me here—that I tried to recreate—to write about. That part that lives within me.

Why do I return? Luca asked. Why do I continually return here? He stopped, turned toward me.

I said, I have the feeling that I've been here before. Strange, isn't it?

Maybe not, he said. You've read about this place, studied it.

Yes.

So you're living the experience you've read about, dreamt of.

Sparrows darted in and out of the stone arcade, landing on the sarcophagi placed along the perimeter of the courtyard garden.

He said, I hope you and Inès will be friends.

Yes. I look forward to meeting her.

He held his arms out to me, then withdrew them, stopping to lean against the stone arcade, looking out into the green courtyard.

Who was this man next to me? Each step rehearsed— reinvented. This walk—a passage reimagined.

And I lost too. If only to establish an I—to remember the actuality of being. Lost in the inhabitable space of fear. Dreamlike and senseless—the nearing of desire. What had I hoped to find?

We entered the chapel. The space—larger than I had imagined. Soaring cathedral ceilings. White stone walls. In the middle—the Altarpiece.

He said, When I was young—still a student—I would sit in front of this Altarpiece. I studied it. I sat here for hours. Who was this artist? Even his name is possibly a fiction.

The crowds reappeared, hovering around the Altarpiece. A mass of bodies. I stood back.

He noticed. He took my hand, pulling me through the crowds to a bench in front of the first panel. A woman wearing earphones got up and moved to the next panel.

Please. Sit down, Luca said.

He sat next to me, pointing to the center panel, to the nighttime image of the crucifixion, to Christ's decaying body, destroyed by disease, riddled with lesions. Grotesque, he said, yet beautiful. Look at the colors. The shapes. The expression.

Christ's body dominated the image, dwarfing the figures around it. Flanked on the right by St. John the Baptist and on the left by St. John the Evangelist. The white-robed Madonna swooning, falling into the arms of St. John.

How do you reconcile this? The grotesque. The strange. The beautiful. The unreal to create the real. The body broken by disease. Destroyed by the act of crucifixion. Green. Gangrene. Difficult to look at. The god-man—man's god, slowly being eaten away at. The dark visage of the landscape. Blankets of color—color fields—green and red—set against a night sky.

Below the panel, the predella. The Lamentation. The dead body punctured, bloody, rotting, surrounded by the Madonna and Mary Magdalene. The body limp. The feet reminiscent of a crow's claws.

Each image a mirror reflecting the next. Tied to

the corners of the room. I entered a landscape of blue and green. Luca sat next to me—tied to that soundless space we had entered together.

These panels haunt me, he said. People dying of an unknown disease. What we know now. The fungus in the rye. The peasants lived on it. Can you imagine? So simple, he said. The monks using these images to comfort them. Miracle-performing, he said.

How did these images comfort the dying? Death romanticized. Degraded. Elevated. The dark nature of the landscape.

Luca said, 1512. He began it in 1512. It took him four years to complete.

And the Jews? I asked.

Why do you ask?

The expulsion, I said.

I don't know, he answered.

Just in my reading, I said. It made me think—some correspondence—the year—1512—those years, perhaps. The reason for their expulsion.

I see, he answered.

I don't know, I said. The plagues. The diseases.

He said, There are references in this piece—to the Jews, to Hebrew. But I've never heard that theory.

He said, Your grandfather—his story. It makes me think. During the war, the Second World War, the Altarpiece was taken by the Germans—to Munich.

Stored there. Restored there. Used once again for healing. Bringing wounded soldiers to it, to pray in front of it.

The image broke open. The sky cloudless. Time warped. The meaning lost in narrative.

And my grandfather continued to write in his diary.

I see the shifting borders continue to elude them—words disappearing on the page.

This piece caught in shifting borders. Taken. Hidden. Displaced. Where had it been when my grandfather came within sight of these borders? Without sight of this or any other sense of how this iconography had been used to conquer and divide.

The bench. The light. The method of display. How you reconcile being here. Outside the moment. What you hear—a memory. The bench—the room—a vast space of aspiration.

Healing and hate. A necessity in conflict.

We sat together. The image before us. In awareness of the silence between us. The question between us, weaving its way through us.

He said, Come with me. Let's go to the other side.

Once again he led me through the crowds, tour groups, elderly couples. Hushed discussions. Reverence.

Why have I come here—to ask what I could not

ask? What will I find? If nothing—then that reason for being remains the same.

Luca pointed to the center panel, the Nativity. To the side of the Madonna and Child—a chorus of angels. He pointed out the green-feathered chorus member. In the back, behind the other chorus of angels. More demon than angel, don't you think? His feathers are peacock's feathers. He has a peacock's crest.

The tour guide motioned for the tour group to follow her to the next room. As they left, I moved closer in.

The feathered creature stood in the back inside a temple with golden pillars. He held a viol and looked upward. The creature's green bled onto the robes of the other chorus members. The green bled onto the panel in the nativity scene. The green of Christ's decaying body. Of death, of rot, of gangrene. And yet his face had an angelic expression.

Set between the Madonna and Child and the temple, a bathtub and a chamber pot. When I moved closer to the panel, I noticed the Hebrew lettering on the chamber pot.

Here, I said. The Hebrew lettering. The lettering that you spoke about.

Yes, he said. Wouldn't that make sense?

I'm not sure, I said. Does it degrade the Hebrew? Its placement there? To associate the language with a chamber pot? To associate a people with defecation, with waste?

Or does it center us on the origins of the child? he said. Where this child has come from.

Luca didn't seem to want to pursue this. He turned my attention to the Annunciation. He said, The Madonna is strange here. Unusual. Depicted differently than by other artists of the time. What do you make of her? Do you think her face is vulgar? he asked. Huysmans called it vulgar. What do you think? Not soft, he said. Aged. Hard. It betrays the notion of innocence. Getting up, he walked to the other side of the room.

Is her face vulgar—and if—will the image relinquish the question? Her face turned away—as if Annunciation is a recognition of anxiety.

Who was the artist who created this? From what time? What place? Driven by what desire? To escape? To please? To acknowledge the brutality of death? What sense of the body mistakes the fragmentation of experience? To discover the end, to arrive at the beginning. The drive toward the unspeakable. How will I remember?

To be in this place—a reworking of dream. A path that led toward a hill. Dogs barking in the distance.

I followed the path the artist created, wandering through each panel—wings opening out, revealing stories—nuanced color. Past each image. Each image a reflection on the nature of darkness. Of each darkness, the reflection of nature.

When Luca returned we moved to the final panel—The Temptation of Saint Anthony. The monsters—bird-men. Man's temptations. The saint fending off the hybrid demons. Pulling at him. Beating him. The rotting gangrenous body in the corner. Bloated. Bloodied. Echoing the feathered creature holding a stick above him. A landscape of exaggerated dream-like colors— blues, yellows, greens. The background of blackened burned-out structures. Fires. The desert sky a pale blue. An unraveling. Of suffering. Of nightmare. Of torture.

Shattering the silence—a man's cane dropped. The room stood still. The crowds turned, frightened.

His. Him. This artist's. And why am I here? A station on a journey. To demons. To a saint. Into. A knowledge of no return. And to here. That fear. This. The connection between this place, my grandfather, Brissac.

I wanted to leave, to get out of this place. But Luca—unable to tear himself away from the images, the colors that compelled him to stay.

I said, I need to leave.

He turned to me, his face questioning. So soon? he asked.

Yes, I said. I need to leave.

I returned to the previous village. The winemaker's house, in the Cour des Juifs—across from number 12, was abandoned. A façade. No one left. An image of a wine cask was carved into the grey stone lintel below the second-floor window. The courtyard hidden in shade. Beneath the ramparts.

Inside the courtyard there was one tree. A water well. A rotting shed. Steep wooden stairs led up to the ramparts.

Next to the winemaker's house a woman stood inside the Dutch doorway of a sky-blue-painted building. Two life-size cardboard figures were propped up in the stone courtyard in front of her. The figures—a man and a woman—wore medieval clothing. He was in knight's armor—she, in a red and yellow peasant's gown. Their faces were cut out, empty, ready for tourist photos. In one hand, the knight carried a sign, pointing toward the museum—in the other, a shield with a six-pointed star.

There was a stillness here. Unusual—distant— veiled. The color of the place distracted me. Held me. The quality of blue-grey, grey-blue remained through and into the aspect of language. Seeking. Language. The difference between Hans and Jean. The divide which collapsed understanding.

A ticket? the woman asked.

I didn't answer. I backed away—though she smiled, seemed kind, and wanted to help.

We'll close soon, she said.

And the winemaker's house?

You can see a part of it. A room—some old wine-making tools. It's connected to the old Thieves' Tower. It dates from the 14th century. If you'd like, I can let you in, she said. To the Thieves' Tower, that is. We'll be closing soon.

The woman leaned on the bottom portion of the Dutch door. She smiled again, exposing deep wrinkles around her eyes. She wore a white cotton sundress. Above her a sign read: *Tour des Voleurs*.

A young family with two children entered the courtyard. The children—a boy and a girl—chased each other. The boy climbed on top of the water well in the center of the courtyard.

Get down from there, the father shouted. The young boy laughed. The father picked him up and swung him around.

The mother asked about the exhibit. The girl ran behind the cardboard figure of the peasant woman, putting her face through the empty space. She stuck out her tongue.

What about the children? the mother asked.

The woman behind the door said, I'm not sure. We

do have a strappado inside—and an oubliette. It's up to you. It may be too much for them.

Thank you, the mother said. She returned to her family. She spoke to her husband. The family then took pictures with the cardboard figures, taking turns, putting their faces inside the empty spaces, mocking the figures.

The family left and I was left alone with the woman behind the door.

I said, I'm not sure I'll go in today.

Of course, she said. We'll be here tomorrow.

We stood there in silence. I looked toward the stone water well filled with red geraniums.

Begins and ends with water. In this the landscape draws through and between the river which divides its inhabitants. How much about this place under the stone façade of the tongue works its way into a promise of redemption?

Movement and stagnation. The repetition of each silence.

What I couldn't say. Echoes in the courtyard. The dislocation of being. How could I begin?

Odd, I said, pointing to the well. The Jews were blamed for poisoning the water? Do you know much about that?

Yes, she said. Around the same time the Thieves' Tower was built. She pointed across the courtyard to an unmarked building. That was the old synagogue.

Is it still in use? I asked.

Oh, no.

And the courtyard? I asked.

I work here during the spring and summer months. When the tourists come.

You're from here?

Near here. The next village—to the west.

As though she anticipated my question, she said, I had a feeling that you came here looking for the synagogue.

Why?

Well, we have many tourists who come here to see this.

You do? I asked.

She said, I think it's in the guidebooks. Many tour groups come here.

There's no one left? I asked.

You mean Jews?

Yes.

She said, I'm certain no Jews have lived here for centuries. Not in this village. I could be wrong.

But why?

She pointed to the Thieves' Tower. Massacred, she said. 500—600 years ago. Why would they come back?

I said, Do you know the name Brissac, perhaps?

She looked down. Thought for a second. When she looked up, she said, I don't believe so.

Of course, I said. For some reason, I believed the family came from this area.

Are you here for long? she asked.

I'm not sure, I said.

Touring? she asked.

Yes, I said. Then hesitated to continue. I said, I'm here because my grandfather fought near here—in the First War. I have his diary. I'm researching the landscape.

So you've come too soon. We're opening a small exhibit—documents from the village—from the Great War. It opens tomorrow.

I'll come back, I said.

I walked to the far side of the courtyard, attempting to memorize each detail of the house in the corner. Why did she point it out? It was nondescript. Faded. Run-down, neglected. Though it had qualities of the other houses in the village—wooden shutters, window boxes. There were no red geraniums in the window boxes. There was no movement.

Everything happens as it should. Each and every moment. Before and after. Language descends into a world you can't capture. That I have come this far only to recognize that what I looked for is what I feared. That I would not find the family. That what was before me—an empty courtyard, a wasted shell—is mine.

Perhaps they're gone. Perhaps in hiding. This and everything before me. Only the name remains. Carved on doorposts. The woman in the courtyard—at the museum—with her white cotton sundress. Her ease, her calm, her sense of control.

When I returned, I asked, Is it true that the colors of the houses signify a family's religion? A red house—or a white?

Not quite. Not a certain color. Usually the colorful houses are the Catholics. The neutral ones—the Protestants.

But that doesn't matter now, does it?

Oh. It's getting worse again, she said.

How so?

The divide, she said.

The divide between whom?

When my mother was a girl she wasn't allowed to date someone from another religion. It's like that here. It had changed, she said. When I was growing up. Now, it's getting worse again.

I wanted to ask her what she meant, but I was afraid to pursue this. I said, This courtyard—do you know the people who live here?

She said, When I was growing up, I was told in school that I couldn't speak the local dialect. I was forbidden. We had to forget that part of our past. So I couldn't speak to my grandmother. She spoke the local dialect—really—a different language. I don't think that she shunned me, only that I grew up in a different generation. I regret that now. I think there were things she wanted to tell me, about her, about her husband. She wouldn't talk about it. It was never mentioned. But during certain times of the year—after he had died—she would eat a different kind of bread. No one spoke about it, of course. But I've always suspected.

Suspected what? I asked.

I believe he was a Jew, she said. No one told us. I'm certain, though.

Your grandmother wouldn't tell you?

Well, we didn't speak the same language, she said. And you? Your family?

I was close to my family. I said. But there's no one left now.

No children? she asked.

No, I said.

It's not too late, she said.

I don't know, I answered. I think it is.

She said, I hope that it's not too painful for you?

It never was. Well, I said, it never had been.

She said, I hope you can return. The exhibit is well worth seeing. I hope you don't mind, she said, I need to begin closing up the museum. She came out from behind the Dutch door. She gathered up the two cardboard figures, moving chairs and taking down signs.

That afternoon we followed the path into a woods of dark green. Cadence of steps—soundless—absent of gesture. The day clearing. The wind rustled the trees.

A woman holding a basket of strawberries watched us from a distance. A group of children gathered, digging in the mud, looking for worms and stones. A bit further on, Luca pointed out the remains of a stone wall—and spoke about the ruins of a castle nearby.

How are we here? The path grows steeper and denser. And further from the children—the village, the ruins. The smell of pine, of beech.

He put his hand on my neck, turning my head to the right. Through the greenery a small waterfall. Hardly a waterfall. But what could you call it? Below us—a stream. The dark green woods. Close. Contained. The difference between here and there. Between here and home. Water. On your face on your body. Let's go down there, he said.

Leaving the path, he pushed ahead of me. Through slush and wet leaves. Pulling branches.

I followed him. I walked without thinking—thinking only about what I could not remember. It took hold—controlling me—forcing me forward. What did I hope to find? What could I lose if I turned back? The cave my grandfather hid in. The artillery. The gas. The inability to move. I couldn't find it. I searched for it. I couldn't find it.

Before I knew it my ankle turned. I fell forward on my knees. The silence of the woods heightening the quiet of my fall.

Luca turned back, laughing. Then came up the hill. He reached forward to pull me up. You're not used to hiking. I can tell, he said.

My ankle felt weak.

Let's take a look. He bent down. He put his hands around my ankle. Maybe I need to carry you.

Absent of time and space memory floats, returning wave-like. Each encounter turns to reflect that which is no longer there.

What you do—what you see—what you feel. How does that matter when the place is here and now? The wind—the trees.

Luca stood up and looked at me until I could not look back. It's not far to the stream, he said.

The problem is that we all have admirers in the islands of eternity. He whispered this in my ear so softly that I'm not sure I understood him. I repeated those words—we all have admirers in the islands of eternity. I repeated them silently. I repeated them as though I knew what he meant. I repeated them as though they made sense.

He brushed away small pebbles in the dirt. He helped me sit down. He said, You seem nervous. He tossed the pebbles into the stream.

The sun beat down. Intermittent waves of cool air. On the other side of the stream, a young family gathered with three children.

Leaves and twigs floated with the current. The air—damp earth. The water the border of eyesight.

Had I gone too far? The act inevitable. The walk, the woods, the stream. Access to betrayal.

He took my hand, turned it palm up.

The locus of possibility. An act repressed. The details detached from being. The forgotten night an inevitable place. He knew this, I think.

Luca lay on his back, closed his eyes.

How much did he know about me? This place? The edge of recognition. Rife with dilemma.

Each encounter—annihilation. The body without weight. The act wordless.

He said, You're lost.

The web strung from the branches of the tree. The boy on the bicycle—now home, the tree trunks peeling with age. Each image a false sense of where I am. Only as if. The never being of self. That you speak of.

I asked him about Inès. He ignored my question. He turned over. Brushed the dirt, drawing images in it.

He said, The best thing about Michelangelo's garden in Umbria is how it maintains traces of wildness. The towns here respond to the nature of civility.

We lay on the banks of the stream. The dirt, the ants, the pebbles washed and shiny. His eyes closed.

I turned onto my side. I closed my eyes. Red ants crossed the sand. My grandmother sat on the balcony. At the motel in the desert. Mountains. Palm trees. The water washed with oil, swirling as I dove under. She, knitting a blanket for each of us. And when she was done, I sat with her, pretending to read a book. Each page I turned took me further into an age of uncertainty. I wanted to feel the rough-cut pages—hand-cut. Diving off the edge of the pool into the filmy water. Warm with. Red ants crawling across my feet. The white sand. Over my feet.

The garden ordered. The flowers planted next to each tree. His garden—a garden of stones. The garden a sign of order. The garden a room of the palace. A room of blue and yellow. Birds landed there.

She didn't question if I understood what I read.

Who did Michelangelo create the garden for? The town? The Medici? Himself? Did he lay each stone in order to convey wildness? Did wildness take over the order of stones?

I sat on the chair next to my grandmother. Trying to remember the feeling—before it slipped into memory.

Luca ran his hand through the water. It flowed across his skin. Come here, he said.

He was angry with me. I could feel it. I could feel how he expected something from this moment. I could see it in his eyes.

Where was I? In a car on a side street? On the banks of a stream? In a cheap hotel by the train station?

Description warrants device. The water's edge. Marsh-like. Hidden. The boundaries of time and space. His arm outstretched, he waved to the children in the water.

He said, Can you forget your first feeling of mortality? He said, We all feel this at some time.

Unarticulated. Words. Laughter. Rose from the hollow of the earth. Echoing in the space around us. Their voices, their laughter. Afternoon sunlight. Shadowed by water. Hidden from view. His breath on my neck.

Suddenly I heard laughter. Now backdrop. What existed outside me? How do I fit into it? No longer responsible. Broken from the earth. The trees. The stream. Broken from the words and laughter. The world was silence. Air cannot speak. If I existed in this moment the past would not haunt me.

I put my head down, leaning on my folded arms. I closed my eyes. When I woke up, Luca was no longer there. The sound of water. Birds. Wind. I looked downstream. I saw him walk along the sandy banks. He looked across the running water to the other side. He stopped, pulled a leaf from a tree growing along the water's edge. He looked at it closely, then put it in his jacket pocket.

The family with children was gone. Three teenagers now sat on the banks on the other side of the stream. One of them waded out into the water. He shouted at the two other boys, beckoning them to join him.

I sat up, looking for Luca. I saw him wandering, his countenance searching. His figure—now an outline disappearing into the greenery.

The two other boys joined the first in the water. They splashed water at each other, laughed, pushed each other, playfully. I felt it on my face—the water, the dampness. The ambient sound of birds.

One of the boys shouted out to me from the stream.

I couldn't understand him. I smiled. Brought my knees closer to my body. The boy waved at me. Shouted again, beckoning me to join them.

I looked downstream again but could not see Luca.

When I turned back around two men appeared on the banks of the river watching the young men in the stream. They wore black t-shirts and combat boots. They stood hidden within the foliage. I don't know how long they stood there watching—waiting. I don't believe the boys in the stream knew they were there—watching them. I don't know if the two men were aware that I watched them. The sound of the moving water, of the birds, of the rustling of the leaves.

The two men emerged, moving toward the stream.

This is how it was. It was filled with violence. And yet, I didn't hear anything. I'm not sure I saw anything. And yet, I'm sure I both saw and heard something. Violence shot through the silence of the afternoon. With the sound of the stream, the trees. The wind. The birds that darted from tree to tree.

The word violence conveys nothing of what I saw—what I believe I had experienced. What I believed I had experienced in my dreams or in my waking state. The day passed in the aura of a figure of the shadow that the trees cast on the dirt and silt. The laughter gone. The sounds gone. Pure silence. Just birds just wind. The persistent wind that rattled the leaves. Dying down into still heat.

Two young men. No. Three. Or, only one? What did they look like? If I were to see them again, could I describe them? Had I seen their faces emerge from the crowds, on the bus, seated behind me? On the trains going south? Could I describe their faces with the accuracy needed to claim their identities?

Their faces drawn in charcoal. One dimensional. Without character. Conveyed in the figure of the silt. For how could faces I could not describe follow me? Pursue me? I dwell on their faces. Faces I could not describe. Did my inability to describe those faces stem from my inability to understand what I saw?

This is how it was. Or this is how it was not. Broken from my vision. The silence now replaced with a noise so great I couldn't think. I couldn't feel. The noise sucked the air. Destroyed it. Suffocating. Spinning. Nothing could live through it.

You cannot describe a violent act. For to describe a violent act is to annihilate yourself. How can you assume that you are innocent of the act that you have just witnessed? If I am to describe this act, I need to assume some complicity. Some part of the whole, some part of the break in time and space to which this act now belongs.

The noise spun throughout the air. It would not let up. How had I arrived here? Broken now from my past. The earth shifted.

The noise stopped. A white feather floating. So small—so delicate. Barely noticeable. It absorbed my vision. Everything stopped. Everything still.

And the boys. If I can't describe the act, how can I describe what happened to them? To tell this story is to commit the crime.

I ran. The image speechless. Movement an act outside myself. Each footstep no longer mine. The image I'd dreamt of. The woods relentless. Branches, leaves, mulch. Sound now—only an image. I ran before I understood I was running. Through damp earth. Thick with branches. The dilemma. Left behind. The woods, my childhood. The woods, my grandfather. The woods of beech and pine.

Their faces hidden, features faceless. Tracking the image that succumbed to the shadow. You, I said. As though the you is the I of the no. The shadows that settled in the woods. The woods that sequestered the notion of boundary that divided the you from I. The image that I can't escape following you as I ran. In dream state absent of dream. In dream state only in dream. The vision is the vision of not what I've seen but what I can't describe.

My shoes dissolved. Rocks penetrated the soles of my feet. My body was not my body.

So, I began again. I ran—floating weightless. Movement as the isolation of time. Suspended. Without breath.

The trenches overgrown. Animals burrowed in the brush.

Describe the sound of cicadas. Of lizards in the undergrowth. Of engines and false wind.

I ran through the woods, lacking the knowledge of what I feared. It was only sensation. My legs scratched and bruised. Past branches. Dead leaves. Trace images floating.

I heard a train in the distance. I slowed down. My body incapable of moving further. The image: a white figure emerged from a black canvas.

Blueberries, lilies, orchids. Flowering yellow. Movement in the earth below me. The shrieks and laughter of children in the distance. I found my way to the white path—marked by the grey stone wall.

I showered. I put on my last clean dress. I re-applied my make-up in the bathroom mirror. My features appeared blurry. I drew a black line around each eye. I put on my red lipstick—wiped it off. Re-applied it again. As though my mouth were shifting, my face changing. Transforming. With no more sense of who I was of what I was. At that moment, did it matter?

It was still early. I went down to the hotel lobby. The desk clerk didn't look up. Two couples sat at a table in the courtyard, drinking white wine. A void. An absence. A silence of the space. It didn't seem right. I left the hotel and walked to the café in the square.

It was that hour between cocktails and dinner. When the world existed in a nether-space of denial. And I envied those people who had purpose and urgency. Some sense of place. Of belonging. There were many tables still open. I sat down at a table on the terrace— within sight of the square. The ambivalence of living between.

The waitress came out. She said, You've been here before.

I'm staying at the hotel up the street.

Is it nice? she asked. I believe it's quite posh.

It's nice, I said. But impersonal.

As are all hotels, she said. I'm planning a trip to the south, she said. It's almost here. I leave tomorrow.

I said, That will be a wonderful escape. Though it's beautiful here, it's far too hot.

She said, Yes. She ran her fingers through her curly blonde hair. Just look. No point in trying to make it straight. She put out her hand to shake mine. She said, I'm Paulina.

I said, Can I get a glass of white wine. A dry white wine.

Of course, she said.

I took out my notebook. Yet another white page. Each word—diminished, unimportant. Disconnected. I pulled out my grandfather's diary—opened it. I thought about the cave—about the journey he would take. But I couldn't make sense of it—of him—of this place—of the trajectory of his life.

He left. He fought. He ended up in a cave.

The darkness overwhelmed me. I could not bridge these lives. His—her's—mine.

A child played in the square. The light changed. The coming months. Spring to summer. The onslaught of despair. How everything changes and I cannot hold on to it.

Unable to abandon here—mired in a desire for the past—for the past that could have been.

I wanted to abandon my things—so that I did not have to face them.

The woman I searched for—my place here—the beginning—a beginning in this valley—now covered

in grapevines—the bodies buried beneath the streets—
to tell and re-tell and then forget. Who was this woman
I wanted to find? What was this history I could not
understand? My grandfather's story? Unattached to any
religion, to any god. And so then. Why did I care? My
childhood. The boy in the square. Rolling in the grass.
Climbing the tree—looking out over the fence. The boy
with a stick, running through the courtyard. Poking at
something. The dog rolling on its side. The light now
changing.

Okay, I said. Okay. But—now—what? But now
where to? What happened in the woods? Do I put it
behind me? Do I bury it? Did it happen? Blurred and
blurring. At what point do I begin to see my fear? My
face in the glass? The rupture between what is here and
what has been? We are stranded. Orphaned. Buried.

Paulina came out, set the wine in front of me. She
said, What are you writing?

I don't know, I said. I don't know.

A carafe of water was placed in the middle of the table between them. It was the first thing I noticed when I entered the restaurant courtyard. The two of them. The table set. The carafe of water. They sat across from each other speaking softly—so softly that those at the next tables could not hear them. He held her hand. Across the table. She appeared animated yet discreet. There was a third place setting between them.

Over time, Luca said, don't things always become clear?

Inès interrupted him. She said, The more time that passes, the less aware we are of what an event means. The less we feel a part of it.

He said, But we gain perspective, don't we?

He looked at me. Smiled. Put his other hand on my shoulder. She pulled her hand away from his. I hope you'll enjoy the food here, he said. This is just the beginning. You'll taste the landscape.

I tried to remember the night before. The details had begun to fade. The red and white checkered tablecloth. The bowler hats hanging above us. How many days had I been gone? Wandering. Finding. Losing. My sense of space of landscape of time. The walk in the woods. The image of the boys—what I saw—what I thought I had seen. Had it happened?

This space, this courtyard, was different. Lights were strung from the trees, between the buildings. White canvas sail shades hung above us. The space glowed in the late-night spring air. A sense of the celebratory. Of the fine. Of all that was and had been missing. Of all that drifted through me during moments of despair. I couldn't lose this moment.

Inès turned to me. And the museum? she asked. The Altarpiece? Luca told me you went together this afternoon.

It's not what I'd expected. I'd imagined the space differently. I hadn't imagined the crowds. I hadn't expected the brutality in the work.

Inès said, Of course not. It's different in person. Reproductions don't convey the power. She looked at Luca. She was delicate, beautiful. But she had a fierce look in her dark eyes. Self-assured. In control. Intimidating.

He said, But you appreciated it?

Yes, I said. Of course.

The young waiter brought us champagne flutes. He left and returned from the sideboard next to us with a bottle, holding it out to us to show us the label. Cremant, he said. One of the oldest vintners in the region. He poured us each a glass.

Luca held his glass out to me.

I took a sip—apple, peach, mineral. I put the glass down but continued to hold on to the thin glass stem.

The waiter then brought out a miniature olive tree set inside a small white planter. He placed it in the middle of the table. Green and black olives hung from the tree's branches.

Luca gestured for me to take one.

I plucked an olive off of the tree and took a bite. Inside, a briny mixture of olive paste.

Beautiful, isn't it? he said.

Inès laughed. She pulled off an olive. Delightful, she said.

He said to Inès, We ran into each other on the street this morning, then walked through the square. There was a parade of bicyclists. The usual parade. The usual procession. Every holiday.

Always a holiday here, she added. Any excuse.

He said, In the middle of the procession, a young boy caught his foot in the spokes of his father's bicycle. No one noticed. The father didn't notice.

She shuddered. Is he okay?

Yes, okay, he said. I'm sure he'll be okay.

I took another sip. I couldn't get the image out of my mind. The boy's foot. The blood. The cobblestone square. The chaos of the morning. How many more times would the image return? From here on. How I wanted to sleep. Go back to my room. I couldn't. I knew I couldn't.

She turned to me, Luca told me so much about

you—about your journey, your book. I'm so happy to meet you.

I nodded. Where to next? Where to?

Inès asked, What made you begin this book? This journey?

I'm not sure. Something drew me to this.

The waiter came back to the table. He asked us if we had made our choices.

I don't know, I said. I haven't had a chance to decide.

Luca said, Let me choose for you. And you, he said, nodding at Inès.

Of course, she said. Go on, she said.

Luca spoke as I spoke. The words confused. The language confused. The food, the ideas. The clarity. A distraction.

I said, I had nowhere to go. I knew I needed to leave. Leave home, that is. At least that's what I had thought. My mother had just died. And I remembered this diary—my grandfather's WWI diary—that my mother had talked about. I had some vague recollection of it. Of her showing it to me. I can't be certain. I just have—had some sense it was important. That I needed to pursue it.

What will you do with it?

I don't know. Not yet.

Will it be a book?

I shrugged. Diminished. And took another sip of wine.

But he was in the Great War?

Yes.

And so you have some sense of its importance here?

I think so.

We're far from the battlefields.

Yes. But not too far, I think.

Well, she said.

I felt myself crumble. As though she could see through me. As though she knew that I was a fraud. My hair. My clothes. My thoughts. Even the way I ate. What did I know about this place? What could I ever know?

Luca interrupted. You'll be pleased with dinner. Everything here is local. Precise detail. The food is art. A minor form, he added. There's a certain intelligence and wit to each dish.

Each image stayed with me. It was true. The grassy battlefields—now deserted—a tourist stop—were far from this place. And yet, not so far. Another form of tourism. The trenches—a curiosity for those who can't imagine. What had he gone through? The space he lived in. The chalky white rock he dug in.

Tomorrow night there's a performance in the square—for the holiday, Luca said.

Inès seemed strained. She looked down at her plate. Fidgeting with her knife. She pulled at her skirt. She looked up, regained her composure and smiled.

The waiter returned with the first course. He placed a white plate of steamed white asparagus in front of me. A second plate of ham and three small bowls of sauces. He delivered a terrine of goose foie gras to Inès along with a small plate of toasts and rhubarb compote. He put a small bowl in front of Luca. Beautiful, Luca said. Look at it—vermicelli with local mushrooms and a poached egg. He lifted the bowl to his nose. I hope you'll have some.

The waiter returned with three glasses of wine—each matched to our respective dishes.

The asparagus was sweet. Delicate. Earthy. The hollandaise—too rich. The quality of velvet.

Luca said, I knew you would like this. I've figured you out.

He likes to collect interesting people. Inès laughed. His personal aviary. What would you call it?

He smirked. He said, She's known me too long. We've worked together too long. She thinks she has the authority to say these things.

She said, Luca looks at everything from a perspective we can't begin to understand. In Luca's world, we're a collection of actors. He orchestrates our moves in a fanciful tableau or play.

Here, he said. Taste this. He handed me his bowl. Inside, the poached egg had broken across the noodles. The flavors mingling in a dark meat broth.

Yes, I said. Very good. Unexpected. The taste lingered. The broth had an unusual quality, almost that of soy. I passed the bowl back to him. He handed it to Inès. She held her hand up to her face, gesturing that she didn't want any.

Luca said, You asked me about a woman—a woman you're looking for. Inès grew up here. She might know.

Yes. I said. And then took another bite.

Who? Inès asked. She held a toast spread with foie gras and compote. Is she connected to the book you're writing?

I'm not sure, I said. I'm trying to find out.

What was the real reason I was here to find her? To know her? To understand why I had to find her? That she may be the last? And I may be the last? And for some reason, I had to find her to understand that.

What is her name? The family name. It's a small village, she said. Certainly, I'll know her—or can find her.

What would it reveal about me? And why not enjoy the evening? The warm weather. The glowing space that spread out before us. Why always this? This moment as a device to prolong the inevitable. The moment— suspended. The quality of muslin. Of fine mesh.

Why had my mother kept this—this news clipping in my grandfather's diary? What had it meant to her? The diary of her husband's father—my grandfather—

his handwritten note in the margins, Brissac, and, this newspaper article on Madame Brissac. Was it a message, a desire—to know her husband—her husband's father? Was it as simple as a question that someone, someday, would need to pursue? Kept in a drawer with other notes, letters, pictures. The others all labeled. She had always labeled everything. Kept precise notes— time, date, place. Yet this small clipping with Brissac's name. No sign, no signal. Perhaps it meant nothing. Something misplaced.

I had no choice. I said, Brissac. Brissac is the family name.

She put down her wine glass. Leaned forward and looked at me. I didn't want to believe that there was something in that look. Something cynical or even sinister. I wanted to believe it was curiosity.

Is it familiar? Luca asked.

She shook her head. No, she said. Not familiar.

Well, she must have some importance for you, he said.

How to articulate what cannot be articulated— what moves us to find things we do not and cannot understand?

I said, My mother placing that newspaper clipping with Madame Brissac's name in it—inside my grandfather's diary—the diary in which my grandfather had written the name Brissac in the margin.

Brissac. Jewish? she asked.

I believe so, I said.

Ah well, Luca said. Okay, he said. So, that's why you came to the old synagogue.

I told him that it was strange—a strange coincidence. Not necessarily to find her. But that when he told me about the exhibit, I was interested. I wanted to see his work.

Certainly a Jewish name, she said. But there are no Jews here, not anymore. I'm quite certain.

I felt her looking at me, with that expression of, so, this is who you are. A curiosity. A strange intrusion. A Jew. And the woman at the bar: never tell anyone who you are.

Luca looked at me, noting my expression. I couldn't read his. But at that moment felt a sense of connection. Was this real—or yet another desire to be?

No more? he asked.

She shrugged her shoulders. I don't know. I don't believe there is anyone left. Well, I'll try to find out something, she said. I'll check around tomorrow.

The waiter returned with the second course—beef tartare, veal with spring vegetables, and a pike soufflé in a Riesling sauce.

Luca again raised his glass. He said, We'll help you find this woman. You're on a journey, he said. I hope we can be a part of it.

I smiled. Once again, I felt sick. The fish was beautiful—airy, custard-like—but floating in cream and butter. And I sat here alone in this space with two people I could not trust but could not leave. This is it, I thought. No turning back now. They know who I am. I picked up my glass of wine.

I asked them if they wanted to go somewhere, get a drink. Inès looked at Luca. He looked back at her. There seemed at that moment a communication between them I couldn't break.

She said, I don't know. I don't think so. I'm a bit tired.

He said, Maybe. He hesitated. I'd better not. I do have to get up early tomorrow. We can walk you back to the hotel.

I told them that I'd be fine. Thanked them for the evening. They each kissed me on the cheek before turning down the street together.

I turned to walk back to the hotel. I made it to the front door. The lights were on inside—but the tables and chairs empty. I didn't see the night desk clerk.

It was a warm night. Humid, sticky. I knew I wouldn't sleep. I turned around and went back to the café in the main square.

I found one empty seat at a small table.

You made it, Paulina said. I'd hoped you'd come back. She sat with two other men at the next table. The older man smiled when I sat down. He said, I'm sorry, I don't speak much English. The younger man smiled. He took a sip from his drink.

You speak well, I said.

Oh, no, he said. I should speak much better. He looked over at Paulina. She speaks well. She can translate for me.

Paulina laughed. Okay. She took a sip from her drink. This is my night off, she said. I can finally relax.

A waitress came out. I ordered a cognac.

The older man said, So what brings you here?

Just traveling, I said. I took a sip of the drink. It burned my throat.

There's a lot of tourism here now, he said. Too many crowds.

Yes, I said. I didn't expect it.

Do you like it here? he asked. He turned his body to face me.

Yes.

I can't imagine why, he said.

Paulina kicked him under the table. Come on, she said. You don't need to be negative.

Why not? he said.

The younger man sitting next to Paulina leaned in to whisper something in Paulina's ear.

She giggled.

I'm retired now, the older man said. I can say

anything I want. Wear anything I want. He pointed to his clothing. He wore shorts and a t-shirt.

Paulina and the young man laughed, continued to whisper together. The younger man also wore shorts—and a tank top.

Paulina said, She's a writer.

I wouldn't call it that, I said.

Come on, she said. I've seen you here with your notebook.

What are you writing? the man asked. He put out his hand to shake mine. I'm Jan. He pointed to the younger man. He's Karl. Karl nodded and smiled, picked up his drink as though to make a toast.

He said, A travel journal?

Something like that, I said.

Tell me more.

There's not much to tell, I said. I've been looking for someone. Someone I thought lived here, somewhere in this village.

Why here?

I said, I believe it has something to do with my mother—with my father's family.

That all seems very vague.

Yes, I said. It is.

Is your family from here?

No, I said. At least I don't think so. But then I thought better. Perhaps we were all from here. At some time. In some moment. In some history. Began here, in some way. From here, from then. Dissolved now. That.

He said, Can you tell me more? I might know this person.

I told him the name. The family name is Brissac.

No, he said, I'm not from here. I live here now. But I don't call this home. I come from the coast, the northern coast. It's beautiful. You need to go there.

Paulina said, I'm leaving tomorrow. For the sea. Oh, to get out of this place.

They're young, Jan said. He pointed to Paulina and Karl. They don't worry. They don't have worries.

At one time I had hope, Jan said. And why shouldn't I? Here we are, sitting in a café, enjoying drinks. Here I am—a warm spring night, sitting outside in this beautiful place. Sipping an Aperol spritz. He lifted his glass, pointed to the red liquor. He pointed to Paulina and Karl next to her. Their tea and rum cocktails. Isn't it all perfect?

I didn't know what to say.

He said, How long are you here for?

A few days. A week. It depends.

I can see you don't know this place. How could you?

You're right, I said. How could I know?

I'm retired, he said. I'm old, he said. Forced to retire. Why?

Why? he repeated. Because this is a fascist country,

he said. I'm old, too old. I can still remember. Those two—he pointed again to Paulina and Karl. They're young. They don't remember what it was once like.

We're not so young, Paulina said.

Yes, you are.

Karl—what do you think?

Karl just smiled. Paulina jumped up and went inside the café. She returned holding two drinks. She placed one in front of Karl—the other for herself.

I'm sixty-three, he said.

That's still young, I said.

Not here, he said. I was forced out. But I have a pension. Every month.

Paulina said, You make enough, Jan.

Well, it has nothing to do with that. At one time I had a good job. They forced me out.

Stop being so negative, Paulina said. You're leaving for the sea tomorrow.

Yes, he said. You need to go there, he told me.

I'll try, I answered.

They're too young to remember, he said. What it was like. Even my aunts. They voted in this government. They lived through the war. They saw what happened. How could they be so stupid? I can't speak to them now. Not anymore. How could they forget?

Paulina said, It's not good what's happening here. It won't happen again. Not like last time.

You see, Jan said. Naïve. Just naïve. The government's going right. It's happening again. It will always happen again. I want to leave, he said. I'm going to leave.

Where? Paulina said. Where are you going to go?

Somewhere south, he said. An island. I don't know. I know I have to leave.

It's not going to get that bad, she said.

It will, he said. You can see it happening. I'll take my pension. Get out of here. Karl will come with me. Won't you Karl?

Karl laughed again. He leaned over to whisper in Paulina's ear. She shook her head.

Jan said, Karl and I have been together for three years. We've made it three years. He's my partner for life. I'll take care of him.

Where will you go? I asked.

I have enough money. It's not much. I know I can find a place somewhere south. Why not live by the sea? Where the people are more open. They're closed here. You never know what they're thinking. You can't trust them. They'll always keep you out. It's going to happen again, he said. He picked up his Aperol and finished the last of it.

I hope I'll see you again, I said.

We're leaving tomorrow—for the sea. We'll return in two weeks. It's beautiful there. You need to go.

Paulina said, No. She has to go to the mountains.

You must see the mountains. Especially this time of year.

No, Jan said. The sea.

Paulina raised her arms in the air—in mock defeat. Okay, Jan, she said. Whatever you say. She looked at Karl. We need to go, she said. Karl is training me in the gym, getting me in shape, getting me ready for the sea. We all live together—in the same building. We're neighbors.

In the ghetto, Jan said.

I'll be back soon, she said.

Jan stood up. Really, he said. You must come to the sea.

Oh, come on, Paulina said. She stood up. Karl followed her. Paulina came over to me, put her arms on my shoulders and kissed me on the cheek. She caught up to Karl and Jan outside the cafe. The three of them walked together through the square before they turned the corner and disappeared.

Hybrid dreams. His. Mine. The quiet of late morning. The sound of children in the courtyard. The trees that cast shadows on his face. Luca said, Can I show you my studio?

We turned down a cobblestone alley that led to a gravel path along the village ramparts.

A mockingbird pecked at a small fruit on the ground. The path—sluggish—dampened by the rain.

A tower stood along the ramparts. Behind us the stone walls of the village—the moats filled with gardens—tomatoes, lettuces, herbs.

The sun was strong now. We sat down on a bench, looking out at the river, at the hills covered in grapevines, at the crumbling castle in the distance. A couple pushed a baby stroller along the other side of the grassy moat leading to the river's edge.

Luca took the diary from my hand. He turned it over. Opened it to June 12. He read: On the train. Riding in a freight car. Passing through fields.

I said, Why am I drawn to this diary? Of this man I never knew? Of this place? Of this landscape? Of this man compelled to write each day—for whom? For himself? For Rose? For his mother? For me? For the son he didn't yet have? For the grandchild he wouldn't know?

He said, Bring this diary with you.

He stood. Held out his hand.

We continued to walk. He linked his arm with mine. Were you ever married? Do you have children?

Married once. Yes. And you?

No time for children, he said. He inadvertently looked over to the couple pushing a stroller through the grass.

Do you regret it? I asked.

No time for regrets, he said.

I told him I wanted to return to the museum to see the Altarpiece.

He told me about the village—the medieval design. He talked about the differences in cities. How they were laid out. On grids—in circular patterns.

Birds squawked. The wind in the trees. The morning becoming day.

This is a small version of a city that spirals—a chaos of intersecting vectors. Angles—which don't resemble angles but threads that unravel.

Each city is a memory. Each memory a village. The village I walk exists in my memory as fear. The streets the courtyards the canal. My consciousness not as home but as place. Entrenched on a stagnant battlefield. Lines buried in the earth. Subterranean lives.

He led me down the main street in the village, past the restaurant we had eaten at the night before last, to a small side street. He pointed to the street sign—named after an artist, he said. Note how each house is painted a different color. We arrived at a blue house with brown shutters. We're here, he said, taking out his key.

I'd like to photograph you, he said. I want you to look mean. Look angry. I've been thinking about that since I first met you on the bus.

I wanted to ask him why. Something held me back. At one time—when I was young—I could understand. When all but myself had been erased. At this moment, here?

We walked down the few steps to the basement studio. The lights were off. Mid-day light entered from street-level windows.

Do you mind if I leave off the lights? he asked. The light is soft now—a bit cool.

I looked toward the light emanating from the narrow windows. I followed him to the back wall.

Above this a wall of birds. Cages filled with parakeets. Cockatiels. Cockatoos. Conures. Macaws. Parrots.

What do you think? he said. You get used to the

chirping. I like it. Especially when I work. Different than music. A kind of music. Birdsong. The original, he laughed. I brought them in last week. Inès thinks I'm crazy. She often doesn't understand these things.

Coffee? he asked. Wine?

The caged birds' wings fluttering. The chirping incessant. Dizzying. His captured aviary. How could he work here in this space? Yet it belonged here, to him. A part of him I could not understand. Somehow I was drawn to that. To this place outside of nature, recreating nature in the abstract, in its ephemeral whimsy and darkness.

Look around, he said. I'll get us something to drink.

Next to the cages—a sculpture. A blue peacock with a serpent's tail, floating, defied gravity, defied its weight. Hovering—suspended in the corner of the room. Part of the series, he said. I just finished it.

I turned to look back at Luca in his makeshift kitchen. He was busy gathering glasses and a bottle of wine.

I could see how this piece, this peacock, emerged here from this space, from this wall of birds next to it. From the isolated moment we existed in together. That moment in time in which the past and the present seem irrevocably tied together. He and I within this absence.

The bird floated. The bird didn't float. This weightless quality—a brilliant conception that could not be defined. Had he invented himself in this light? In this way? Or did he believe it?

How do you do it? I asked. I motioned to the sculpture.

He said, Can I give away all of my secrets?

Secrets?

This idea of reflection, he said. Who we are. How we create art of the absence. As an artist do I have a responsibility to our world? Even to our country's past? Must I live under that shadow? What if we were to enter a room with a taxidermied baboon and someone called that art? Do you abandon all reality? Do we abandon morality? Simple good taste. What do you think?

He hadn't answered me. Not directly.

He returned from the kitchen with the bottle of white wine. With two glasses. Set them down on a drafting table. He poured us each a glass. Here, he said.

He raised his glass. Clinked mine.

The wine burned my throat.

He smiled. Let's just enjoy the afternoon, he said.

We stood in the middle of the studio. A large white workshop. He pointed to the far corner of the room, to a sculpture of a goat with yellow horns, a swirling orbit, spiraling, circus wheels in place of feet.

I sipped the wine.

How do you redefine the natural world? he asked. Must we act out our fears? Must we write them?

I will find you, I said.

What? he asked.

Nothing, I said. Something I'd written on a scrap of paper.

Did I get too close? he asked. Must you write out your fears?

Something like that, I said. Yes.

Here, he said. Let's see the rest. Let me hold your glass for you.

He brought me to another corner of the room. He said, When we drink we lose sight of what's real and what's illusion. Isn't that what it's all about? He pointed to another sculpture—what appeared to be two thin feet—a man's—a woman's? The veins protruding. The large toe deformed—a blue eye.

I'm not sure where it will go, he said. I just need to keep working. The piece will find its form.

Your show opens soon, I said.

Yes, he answered. We don't have much time. He handed me back my glass of wine. Let's drink, he said. Until we forget. Isn't that the point, he said. So that we can no longer tell the difference. Carnival, he said.

Inès set up this studio space. I've had to make it feel like it's mine. I have a similar one at home. At first it was difficult—to find my bearings—here in this village. Inès can be a bit overbearing. I'm sure you've noticed. Now I find it's easier to work here. The city is all business. This is my retreat.

He said, I've divided my studio into seasons. I'll take you on a tour. Come look at this, he said. I'm particularly fond of this one. He took me to the far side of the studio. Past the window—flickering light and dark. Shadows. Footsteps in the street.

Summer, he said. He gestured to the sculpture in front of us.

At the castle walls moss covers stone. The knight stands in a mud trench. He wears a cross on his head.

Luca said, I brought you here first. It should be of interest to you. To your work. To your search for your grandfather.

I said, The image is haunting. A cross, a knight, a castle, the earth.

Isn't this our world?

I said, I once read somewhere that the history of warfare was that of man getting closer to the ground. From knights on horses to men dug deep in trenches.

Yes, he said.

Here, I said, the dreamlike vision takes over the horror.

Or does it? he said.

It's not the animal world, I said.

Or is it? Isn't the man the animal? You're too far

113

removed from that—from that concept. From that feeling. Here we are in this quaint village.

What's this about? This moment? This encounter? Only in reflection. Years later, perhaps, I will understand why I am here. At this moment. With this man. Unless I forget. Will I rewrite this moment ten years, twenty years from now? With any understanding of motivation. Of desire. Am I writing my destiny? But why here, now? How long have I held on to this memory—or is it a dream? With what intent? To understand? To forget? To believe that connection is the outcome or the demise?

This is Spring, he said. He took my hand again and brought me to the opposite corner of the studio. A raven growing out of a desert cactus—set on a tufa rock. I love the desert, he said. That's where I first found myself, found my vision. When I was young I went to America. I hitchhiked across the country. Found mescaline. Immersed myself in native culture.

What sudden paranoia? Or was it? What I could and could not see before me. He took me to Winter, to an all-white stone Neolithic structure teetering on the edge of balance.

He said, My Stonehenge. My homage to winter rites. To the deepest blue of night. He turned back to see my reaction. He said, I told you earlier that I wanted you to look mean.

I don't understand, I said.

I want you to look mean, he said laughing. Here, show me your meanest expression. He put his face close to mine. I want to see that darkness. I know you can do it. That's the part of you I want to capture.

What did he intend? Why did I go there? Did it exist within me? Could it? Or was he at that moment trying to find himself? The consequence of that meanness. His meanness written through me, seen through me. Expressed through me to reveal himself, to revel in the conquest of what he had achieved. To reveal myself to reveal what he wanted me to be.

He came too close to me. He said, Let me pour you another glass of wine.

He led me to a sculpture of a woman. Her arms crossed hid her human nakedness. A muslin cloth wrapped tightly around her legs. Protecting? Holding them? Binding? Making of them a root? Exposed? In air. Twigs with red and gold leaves grew out of her dark curly hair—twisting—extending outwards—falling around her. The fall colors bleeding onto the tone of the sculpture's skin. Her eyes—averted from the viewer's gaze—looked aside.

What do you think? he asked.

How did he see this woman? How did he perceive her?

The body yields to the prospect of change. To return to chaos. To return to the establishment of being. The image becomes.

He wanted to know about my life. About my interests. About my desires.

I wanted to tell him that the day and night no longer have meaning as distinction. False breaks in the night sky.

But I did not tell him these things.

He said, A magazine is doing an article on me, on my work, on my sculptures. They need a photograph. What do you think? Can you shoot that for me?

I don't know much about photography, I said.

You don't have to, he said. I'll set it up.

In front of us a figure of a wolf's head—six feet wide—its jaw open—howling—exposing half-canine-half-human teeth. The grey fur ears were cocked forward toward the viewer. The fur transformed from the ears downward into a flesh-like skin tone that surrounded the creature's strangely human eyes, eyes that looked out from the side of its head, watching me. Studying me.

I'll set it up for you, he said.

A wall of raised forms. Barely discernable. Faces emerging from the surface.

He said, I just need to change my shirt.

I touched the sculpture. The surface was cool, rough.

He returned holding a red shirt. How does this look? he asked.

Dark. Cloud. He walked across the sky. Without any expectation for change or loss. He moved toward me. I stepped back, leaning against the table. Papers fluttered soundlessly. Birds chirping. Incessant. Never ask the ruin what precedes the mark of chaos. Disintegrating. Crumbling. He stepped toward me. I felt his breath on my face. His shirt had the odor of the street—the alleys—the trolley cars. The bakery. The last woman he'd kissed.

My arms are fragmented—aloft in the circle he has dreamed—the ring of animals filtered through the unearthed landscape between consciousness. He put his hands on my shoulders. I could not move. He. You. I. Becoming it. You—he—across the sky. Blurring shapes, morphing into the perspective of trees rocks mountains cactus. Night. Streams. The pond where you watch your reflection seep into mud.

He said, No need to worry about light or distance. I will do it all for you. Really, he said. No need to worry.

He changed his shirt from grey to red. I think it will work.

He said, It's ready. He climbed back inside of the sculpture, inside of the gaping mouth.

A jack-in-the-box, he said. A creature emerging from the depths. What I have unleashed. He said, Goodness. Evil. The ambivalence of morality. He laughed. I'm ready when you are. We look down from this height to the sky-less depths. You can't be afraid, he said.

I took the photograph. I took it again.

About what? The image on the wall. Its persistence. Its tired reluctance to yield to the convention of change. Each day the same image eating away at the understanding of movement. Or was I wrong? Is this movement?

I turned to the sculpture of the naked woman.

I told him I wanted him to give me permission to forget myself.

He went in the back of the studio, back to the wall of birds. He opened a drawer in a metal cabinet, rifling through its contents. He pulled something out and came toward me. He said, Look. This is for you. This is yours.

What is it?

A mask, he said.

It was a small elaborate creation. The cut-out eyes surrounded by gold leaf. From there, peacock feathers—iridescent—blue, green—variations of pink and white, the tips of the feathers highlighted by black—covered the mask, as though displaying the bird's train, moving upwards from the eyes, creating a delicate crown, the plumage layered from the eyes down until it met the grey bird's beak.

I want you to wear it, he said. He came closer to me, holding the mask out to me.

I moved away from him.

Here, he said.

I moved toward him.

You see, he said. I knew you needed to look mean. He said, Let me put it on you. He reached toward me holding the mask up to my face. This way, he said, your meanness will be disguised for you.

I took the mask from him, holding it up to my face. But I could not feel the meanness in me, the meanness that he wanted from me. That darkness he sought. I felt the cold paper-mâché material, sensing the gesso that bound the feathers to it. I looked through the eyeholes to Luca. He stood close to me.

He said, What do you think?

I could not answer him. As though the mask had

stripped me of my voice. Of any logical way to respond. Of any way to see.

I took off the mask. I handed it back to him.

What did I want from him? What sense of ego did he reinforce? The promise of something I could not quite achieve. As though it could come from outside me, bridging the experience that fulfilled my desire. He told me that when you fly at 30,000 feet and look below you, you are in a theatre. The distance the representation of the desire for self. He asked me to reveal my darkness.

I walked up the stairs entering the image following the scene—as narrative.

The distance between the notion of self and the representation of the body. So separate from and distant from the physical form.

Perhaps there was only one image on the wall.

I needed to leave. I needed to go back to the hotel.

I stepped out into the street. I turned back to close the door. I looked down. My hands had become branches. They had become hybrid creatures.

In the center of town, just past the fountain, a small shop sold confitures—jams, candies, herbs, soaps. Emeline, the woman who ran the shop, said, I go into the woods to find wild herbs. During the winter, my husband and our son dry the herbs and make the preserves with fruits from our farm. In the spring, when the tourists arrive, we open up our small shop. I run the shop. My husband runs the farm. During the week, our son visits the nearby villages, selling our products at open-air markets.

I asked her how long she had lived here. She waved her arm, making one of those gestures, such as, oh, now, how can you ask that? Before history. Her parents, her grandparents, and so on. Before history, she said.

It was a small shop. Floor-to-ceiling shelves filled with products they had grown and harvested—oils, vinegars, dried flowers, teas.

She recommended the rhubarb and the black cherry preserves. Or, she said, the pinot gris, which goes beautifully with foie gras or cheese. Take a sample. She handed me a small plastic spoon and encouraged me to try the jam. She wiped her hands on her red apron.

I tasted it. Sweet—but delicate.

Try this one made from pinot noir.

I took the spoon. Sweeter.

How long are you here? she asked.

A week, I said. Perhaps two.

She pointed to the small bags of dried herbs she thought I could take home and enjoy.

I picked up one of the bags.

Wild garlic, she said. You can add it to grilled lamb.

And this one? I asked.

Tarragon, she said. For salads.

I said, I'm not sure what I can carry. I'm traveling.

Oh, but of course, she said. The preserves are very heavy.

I put the bag of herbs back on the shelf. I said, You must know everyone in this village.

She shrugged. It's small here. Yes. We know almost everyone.

She pointed out the soaps—on the shelf next to the dried herbs. I lifted an olive-green soap. She said, It's a scrub—good for the skin. She gestured as though she were washing her arm.

The shop was hot, humid. And I found myself growing impatient. I wanted to be there. I wanted to leave. I wasn't sure where to go.

Does it get too quiet? I asked. In the winter?

We have our work, she said.

Yes. Of course.

But around Christmas, she said. The place is full.

Too full. Have you visited here at that time of year? There was a long pause. Oh. It's terrible, she said. Too many people. The streets are full. She took out a paper from behind the cash register. Here, she said. A list of all of the products—with translations.

I took the paper. I would collect it. Put it in my purse.

Or maybe you'd like these. She pointed to another bag filled with small dried flowers. We collect these flowers for tea. After you boil the water, take ten flowers and let them steep in the water for ten minutes. It's very good for you. She pointed to her stomach.

The shop—an almost too perfect semblance of country life. The woman in the red apron. The local products arranged on the shelves.

I purchased the herbs and flowers. I told her I would return for the market. I hoped I would see her again.

Yes, she said. Please do.

I was about to leave the shop when I turned back around. I said, Do you know a family named Brissac? A woman—an older woman with the surname Brissac?

She thought for a minute.

I don't know, she said. A friend? she asked.

No, I said.

She said, The name sounds familiar. She looked around the shop. Oh, but I'm not sure. I'm not sure I know anyone with that name. Maybe my husband will.

I'll come back, I said. I'd love to buy more of your

products. But I'm not sure how much more I can fit in my suitcase.

It was early afternoon. I thought I'd find Luca at the old synagogue setting up the exhibition. I opened the outer wooden door. It was unlocked. I went through the entrance which led to the inner sanctuary. Luca wasn't there. Inès wasn't there. The space was empty except for the sculptures placed throughout the room. I walked through them to the front to the raised platform to the remnant of the Roman tile wall. I walked through the light that filtered in from the windows of the upper gallery. It was peaceful. Quiet. I tried to imagine how this space was once filled, with men, with boys. The women in the upper gallery. The sounds of music and chanting. Words I wouldn't understand. I heard the Mendelssohn—the music resonating within the empty space.

I passed through the doors and up the stairs. I sat down on a wood chair along the side of this upper gallery. When I looked down I saw my grandfather in the front of the room, part of the boys' choir. But not here. Somewhere. Somewhere in his new home that he wanted to find. It was Yom Kippur. They had just finished the morning service. The cantor told the choir to go home and eat so that they'd have strength. To break God's written commandment to fast. My grandfather didn't return for the afternoon service. He wanted never to return. A faith, broken.

I covered my face with my hands. I covered my eyes with my hands. I wanted so badly to see.

I returned to the café in the square—just past the fountain. The tables on the terrace were empty. Inside, a few elderly men gathered, talked loudly. Laughing. Drinking white wine. One of them held on to a leash with a golden retriever. The man let go of the leash. The dog ran to me, nudged my leg with its wet black nose. He rolled over on his back.

The woman behind the bar asked if I needed something.

I said, Can I sit outside? Have a glass of white wine?

She motioned for me to sit down. She would bring me my wine.

I took out the package Emeline had wrapped. Placed the packets of herbs and flowers on the table. Perhaps I would leave them on somebody's doorstep. A gift from a stranger. The parties my mother would give. Roasted lamb on the grill.

I took out my notebook, my pen. I drew a square and then circles. And then more squares. The waitress brought me a wine. Setting down the check, she walked inside.

The sky turned cloudy. Light clouds. No threat of

rain. One woman crossed through the square, entering the central government building across the street. Was this experience, here and now, or just an aberration?

A group of bicyclists approached from the main street, stopping outside the café. They took off their helmets, set their bikes against the stone wall, then took a table in front of me. When the waitress came out, they ordered beer.

Slowly the world filled. With images and sounds. Children gathered in the small park down the street from the café.

The waitress returned. I stopped her, ordered a salad.

How I used to enjoy eating alone—those moments of watching, of eating, of listening.

A short while later a man, a woman, and a young child entered the square, sitting down at the table beside me.

The waitress brought me the salad.

When I turned around I noticed the light through the branches, the isolation of the village streets, the wild gardens that lay beyond the city gates. Time had stopped and, in it, the landscape has been torn free from its surroundings. How could that be? Impossible, isn't it? This place, this terrace, these trees—just a momentary feeling. It's all connected, isn't it? To the walls next to it. The apartments, the closed windows lined with flower boxes. The empty courtyard. The fountain. The darkness that contrasts with the light on this terrace.

To escape here would be to escape experience and didn't I love that experience? Even in its worst moments. To live at this moment, to feel it all, see it all. Living my life, my mother's, my grandfather's. To see it for them, with them, without them. The grape-covered hills, the broken castle in the distance. The river that flowed its way through and around the village walls. The green flickering light. As I sat alone, sipping the white wine, the laughter, the voices surrounding me, the family at the next table, speaking, perhaps about the food, perhaps about their work, perhaps about their children in a language I couldn't quite understand. All directions pointed to the persistence of the inevitable. I had come this far.

A blank page. That's what's before me. The night a recognition of what I can't explain. How this page whitens. The sound. The image. The sense. My arms feel limp. The prickly feeling of what I can't feel. In the midst of the crowd, the water fountain. Lit in the night. A full moon. Red flowers in the windows. Hung from the light posts. The medieval sundial pushed back— 500—600 years ago.

We left the hotel tipsy. Drunk. A little off balance. Laughing. Weaving our way down the cobblestone streets. Luca in the middle. Inès and I on either side. His arms around our waists. We didn't speak. Past the café. Into the square.

Let's wash our feet, he said.

What? Inès asked.

A custom, he said.

Come now, she said. I don't know that one.

Here, he said. Let me take off your shoes.

I told them that when I was young I wandered. Wandered from country to country. No real sense of where I was or where I was going.

So, you've returned to do the same? Luca said.

I said, I ended up in Northern Spain. There was a

weeklong festival. Bullfights. Drinking. People in the cafes. Chaos everywhere. In those days, I craved that.

We all do that sort of thing at that age, he said.

On the last night of the festival—early morning—I fell asleep—finally—in a plaza on the outskirts of the historic town. I fell asleep on the grass next to a fountain. I had met three Scottish men. We had spent the night drinking, then wandered the streets until we stopped at a grassy spot. I said, I haven't thought about that in years. When I woke up I realized that I was in the middle of a roundabout. Cars honking, drivers shouting, passing us at furious speeds.

I sat down on the edge of the fountain. Luca took off my sandals. He handed them to me.

I said, I haven't felt like this in years.

He said, I told you I wanted you to look mean.

I couldn't answer.

Inès said, Alas—you want everyone to fight against their natural selves.

No. I want them to be their natural selves.

Okay, she answered.

Rockets sounded in the distance. Red and white lights flashed in the sky. Luca said, We should go down to the river.

Not barefoot, Inès said. She bent over to put her shoes back on.

I told him that he could wash my feet.

Aha, he said. So, I will.

He cupped his hands and put them in the fountain, then sprinkled the cold water over my feet. The water felt good. Refreshing in the humid night air.

Inès said, Ridiculous.

Look at her face, Luca said to me. She's the one that looks mean.

Distant rockets. The night beginning. Flashes in the sky. Imminent now. The crowds would return. Where was Madame Brissac? Was she here—somewhere in this village? Hiding out? Or in the countryside? In a small farmhouse? But I didn't want to think about that now. About why I was here. About what I had to do.

You're too afraid to look mean, Luca said.

That's not true, I said.

Inès left—walked to the far side of the square. She took out a cigarette from her purse, lit it. Leaned against the stone wall.

Don't worry about her, he said.

I'm not, I said.

Let's imagine she's not here.

At first a procession—a small procession—ten men wearing black bowler hats, black jackets, black jeans. They stopped just beyond the fountain. They didn't turn around. They stood stone-faced—as if in a military procession.

I looked toward Luca. I didn't see Inès. Perhaps she was still leaning against the wall, smoking her cigarette.

Luca handed me back my sandals. I put them on. My feet damp with water, sticky with humidity.

A light came on in a window across the square. The windows opened. A man leaned out—waving a giant key. Two women emerged beside him, holding wine glasses.

What does that mean? I asked.

Luca shrugged.

The men in bowler hats moved forward, passing us. They stood in unison just beyond the fountain.

Next, a group of drummers dressed in long white smock coats with pink fur collars entered the cobblestone square. They wore black sunglasses. They had drums slung over their necks. They tapped the drums as they moved at a measured pace down the street.

Luca took my hand. We should move to the side, he said.

But it's meant to be festive? I asked.

Of course, he said.

We moved away from the fountain. Leaned against the stone wall. More villagers arrived. Still, I couldn't see Inès. Such a small square. Where could she have gone?

Two figures wearing fuzzy red wigs and white masks

with deformed faces followed the drummers. The masks had twisted red lips. Large teeth, protruding, jagged. Enlarged red clown noses. These two were followed by figures with green wigs and twisted mouths. Red clown noses. Again, their teeth protruded beyond their garish red lips. Grotesque figures. Figures that had little to do with nature, little to do with the natural world.

There was a slow solemn quality to the parade. Silent, funereal—a strange juxtaposition with the images before us.

Why? I asked. Why the grotesque?

Why the grotesque? he repeated. He stepped back. Thought for a second. The cycle of birth—life—death—decay. The beautiful in the grotesque. The grotesque in the beautiful. This is how it's always been. Don't you see that?

I said, yes, I guess I do. But I didn't. Only a fleeting sense of what was before me—more instinctual than logical.

These are masks, he said. These degradations are no longer abstract. Abstraction is reversed. Now reduced to an image we can understand. The grotesque. The vulgar. This is it. Here, now, before us. Who we really are. Once you put on the mask you no longer need to hide. Your inner self is revealed. He moved forward—looking toward the wall where Inès had been.

In an instant the square transformed, shifted into an unrecognizable space of sound of movement. The night erased. Remade. Reconfigured.

Intermittent rockets followed by fireworks illuminated the sky above us. Multi-colored lights—red, blue, white—signaled the shift—illuminating the orange and yellow buildings in the darkening night. Crowds gathered as if they had been there all along, disguised by the night and sound—families with small children. Groups of teenage boys. Old people. Couples holding hands.

The rockets were ceaseless. My chest grew tense. It was difficult to breathe.

A group of horn players dressed in black entered the square, playing folk music, dancing as they played, laughing, throwing confetti at the crowds who gathered around them. One of the players roamed through the crowd swinging women around, kissing them. He came toward me. I backed away. He came closer. He grabbed my arm, spun me around, trying to dance with me. I couldn't move, frozen. He laughed—taking delight in this—as though that's what he had wanted. He let go of my arm, then kissed my cheek. He slapped Luca on the back, then returned to his group.

Drummers followed the horn players, stopping in the middle of the plaza. They formed a drum circle—

oscillating between tinny sounds and regulated deep rhythms. The air now heavy with the smell of smoke.

Luca returned to stand next to me. The world spun. Despite the open square, the space closed in on me. The crowds, the sound, the flashing lights. I wanted to wash my body, wash my face. Why had I come here?

Luca pointed to the next float—a carnival cart pulled by three hunched figures dressed as witches wearing dark brown wrinkled masks and red and white checkered skirts with checkered scarves on their heads. With one hand, they pulled the float—with the other, they held straw brooms, shaking them in the air. They looked each way as they pulled the cart down the cobblestone street into the square. Once they arrived in the square—just beyond the fountain—they stopped. On top of the float a witch stirred a steaming iron cauldron placed over a roaring fire surrounded by twigs. Behind this witch stood three more witches holding brooms.

Luca said, The village of witches. Since the Middle Ages.

Here? I asked.

He said, The same history as in your country—no doubt. They're mocking, of course.

The witches gathered together. They formed a circle—chanting—the sound, dark and rhythmic—the insular language impenetrable.

At that moment Pulcinella came running down the street. He wore a white smock and white hat. His black mask had a beak-like nose. He swung a giant stick. He shouted at the witches. They hissed back at him. He swatted each one in turn with the stick. They shook their brooms at him—made gestures as if to say— we're putting a spell on you. Pulcinella persisted. He ran through and around them, swatting them with his stick. Eventually they cowered. Ran to the side of the cart.

Pulcinella looked around at the crowd—took a bow. The crowd applauded. More rockets sounded. He walked around the float, looking up at the witches on top—threatening them with his stick—bowing to the crowd.

Little bird, Luca said. The rooster, he said. The Pulcinella—my favorite character. I want to do a series of figures based on him.

A man on horseback, dressed as a soldier, pulled a cart behind him. The cart stopped just behind the witches.

The witches screamed when they saw the float behind them. They shook their straw brooms. They raised their arms in the air. They scurried around on top of their float.

I couldn't discern what the float was about. On it—a papier-mâché figure. I told Luca that I couldn't make out the figure. He said, Let's get closer. He pulled me through the crowds. I held his hand. Parents held their children. Some sat up on their fathers' shoulders.

When we got closer we saw the figure of a man, a man with an oversized hooked nose. He was dressed in a suit and had a cap on his head. The figure, dragged by its neck, hung by strings from a bar. The bar, the semblance of the gallows.

But it couldn't be, I said.

Luca didn't answer.

I didn't know how to read his reaction. Was it paranoia?

Another float came into the square. It stopped behind the horse-drawn cart with the papier-mâché figure. Men dressed in black, with beards and hats and glasses. Long sideburns. They had masks with big noses. They leaned on the side of the cart, holding packages—what looked like books and bags with bread. On top of the float was a large fabric banner. Large letters written in red across the banner. I couldn't translate.

What does it say? I asked Luca.

He stopped. He seemed unsure.

What does it mean? I asked.

He said, The last ones are leaving.

Another float followed. Men dressed in hot-pink oversized costumes—with protruding stomachs. Pink fur hats. Masks with beaked noses. Wearing money belts. Money bags strewn at their feet. One man smoked a cigar—a rat perched on his shoulder. Music blasted. The men danced—and sang to a song—the melody reminiscent of Hassidic music. But the words were muffled. They danced and laughed as the float made its turn into the central square by the fountain.

Beside the float, men dressed as Nazi SS soldiers carried metal canisters with labels—the words Zyklon B printed in red.

Was it what I had imagined? What I had thought? The nightmares of my youth. The maze of hidden corners—the dark woods. Absent of all sense of time and space. The forgotten night.

The crowds cheered. Children laughed. Couples kissed.

And then—all still.

Pulcinella—motionless—watching the images before him—the floats—the revelers in the square—those images that echoed the silence of the square.

Was it silence? Was it only the silence I felt in the midst of a scene I could not comprehend?

As if the world needed to shift, Pulcinella resumed chasing the witches with his stick. The witches didn't move. As if on cue, as if rehearsed, they screamed, pushing him back with their brooms. The crowd broke out in laughter. The music started again. The fireworks, the drums. The men dressed in pink resumed dancing and singing.

Two of the men dressed as Nazi soldiers dragged a girl through the crowd. She was young—perhaps 16. She had long dark hair and wore a sundress. They carried her to the witches' cart. The witches parted to make way as the girl was lifted up onto the cart by the other witches. One witch on top lifted the lid on the black cauldron. They lifted the girl in the air.

The witches on the cart harassed the young girl. They poked her with their sticks. They danced around her.

The cauldron continued to boil. They held on to the young girl.

The witches howled. They lifted the girl in the air. The crowds laughed. Mocking the witches. The sounds, the images. The rockets went off. They dropped the girl. She fell into the cauldron, screaming.

The witches stood still. In shock—incapable of understanding what they had done. Then, they fled. They jumped down from the cart, dispersing, running through the streets.

We were speechless. We couldn't move.

A piercing cry. Silence broken. The girl on the cart screamed out. A couple ran up onto the cart to retrieve her. It was too late. Too late. The world exploded. A chaos of sound of violence. No sense of what had happened when—and at what moment. Crowds running in every direction—but what had direction meant?

Luca grabbed my hand. Let's go, he said. Don't wait.

He pulled me through the square, through the shouting crowds. I looked back. He shouted, Don't look back! A man knocked into me. He didn't turn around. Bodies brushed against me. A blur of bodies. Of motion.

Follow me, Luca said.

We were at the edge of the square. A torch-carrying mob marched toward us from a side street—from the direction of the old synagogue. The men wore white masks—they wore black shirts and jeans. Formally, slowly, ritualistically, they walked down the narrow street that led to the square. They chanted. A slow guttural sound—premeditated. Angry.

What are they saying?

What are they saying? Luca repeated. Now, Luca said. Now, now, now.

We stopped. Shock—fear. The force setting in on us stronger than that which propelled us to move.

The men crowded into the center of the square—in front of the government building, holding their burning torches, chanting, Now. Now.

Let's get out of here, Luca said. Back to the hotel.

I couldn't move.

You need to come.

He didn't move. I didn't move. We stood still. In the corner of the square. In front of the café.

A man at the front of the mob went over to the

witches' cart—now abandoned. The girl now gone. Abandoned. Everything here—abandoned.

He lifted his torch above his head. He shouted, Now, now, now. He flung his torch onto the cart.

At first nothing. And then it happened. The cart caught fire.

The mob of men broke free—dispersing, running with their torches through the square, down the side streets of the village. A car next to the café exploded in flames. The air darkened, filling with smoke. The SS men ran toward the shops in the square—smashing windows.

Sirens. Lights flashing. The lights mirroring the fireworks.

Tear gas, Luca said. There's going to be tear gas. We need to get out of here.

We turned down a side street. A man with a torch and a bat broke the glass in the bakery shop window. He threw his lit torch through the broken glass.

Luca said, Don't look. Don't think about it.

Four more men in white masks came running down the street with bats. They smashed the windows of an apartment building. Glass shattered across the street. The street—a landscape of fragile construction.

Luca stood apart from me. Who was he? Why was I here? Why were we here together? I watched him stand on the side of the street—against the stone wall.

I imagined him a fixture in this place. The road—a surface of unreality broken with the movement of time and place.

He didn't so much signal me to move as he signaled me that this couldn't be happening. Was this signal what I felt or what I had some sense of remembering?

Behind us one of the masked men pulled a young boy out into the street. He left the boy in the center of the square, then ran back toward us, taking a bat and smashing in the windows of the café behind us.

The SS men gathered the pile of books from the float of Orthodox-dressed men. They threw the books from the float into the center of the square. Then poured the liquid from the canisters labeled Zyklon B. One man shouted, Stand back. He threw his torch onto the books. The paper ignited. Burst into flames. Black soot rose. Drifting in the air—falling. Falling around us. The letters falling. The paper eviscerated. Covering us. In our eyes in our hair. On our clothing, our bodies.

Luca took me back to the room in the hotel. I wanted him to leave. He needed to find Inès. She would be fine, he reassured me. This was her village.

He said, I want to stay with you tonight.

I said, I want to be alone.

He didn't say anything.

I rehearsed the actions I would take—checking the lock on the door, looking out the window to the courtyard, waiting for light. How often I had done that—each night. With the first sign of light, I would close my eyes.

He said, Let me stay with you tonight.

That's okay, I said. I'm fine. I'm fine, I said.

He leaned in closer.

I moved away from the door, sat down on the edge of the bed.

He followed me. He said, I want to stay here tonight.

I said, Maybe you should go—see Inès—make sure she's okay.

She's fine, he said. He sat down on the bed next to me.

I'm tired, I said.

Of course, he added, moving closer to me.

I said, I want to leave this place. I need to get out of here.

Leave? he repeated. Where will you go?

I don't know, I said.

But you'll miss my exhibit.

I looked away.

What about your book?

I'm at a dead end. It may not happen.

Of course it will.

I didn't believe him.

Again, he moved closer, leaning in toward me.

Because I don't know how to describe the events that followed—the light from the street—the sky, the moon—fragments of night—the isolation of the room—of the space—the blue curtains—the image on the wall—a drawing—a Henry Moore—woman and child—the oak-wood floor—the floral-painted ceiling beams—I'm left with those moments that reveal my faulty memory—that reveal the way in which memory is burdened by pain. That reveal not so much the loss of memory but the inability to exorcise that pain through words.

His body, his jacket, his body odor. The outline of the woman—the outline of the child. Broken apart. Her eyes looking at me. The child—an outline—with us—without us. Through the sheer curtains—the courtyard. The memory disguised.

I moved away from him.

I don't belong here, I said.

Why not? he asked.

I don't know, I said. I can't do this.

Give yourself time. Forget about tonight. Forget about what happened.

How can you say that?

He said, Why won't you come near me? All this time. You won't come near me. He placed his hand on my lap.

I said nothing.

He said, All this time.

My image reflected in the window through the gaunt presence of light—the sheer curtains that gave way to distorted vision. The night will not leave me. How did I arrive here?

I have tried to write about this moment. Each time a failed attempt. The music I heard—a vague recollection of the moment of fear I did not seek but found myself driven to—a result of that movement toward the moment I could not escape. Everything seen through light—through birdsong—through the absence of light and birdsong—through the lyricism that hid my intent. I was left with the inability to speak to act to shift the course of events.

I had not wanted to make myself a victim. I had not wanted to make him a villain. There was little ground— little movement—little space for ambiguity.

He came closer. He took my hand. He placed it on his lap.

I could not feel his hand. I felt his body—the way his body smelled. Had I been too open—or perhaps, too cautious—stranded here—between—the nuance of experience?

He said, All of this time. Why nothing? he said. Why nothing?

I didn't know what to say. Had I been wrong? I didn't answer. I looked over at the drawing of the mother and child.

He followed my gaze. He said, Forget about tonight. He said, You will.

He took my hand again. Pressed it against him.

Was this violence? A violence directed at me. Or a violence directed at all of us. I don't know—when he undid his pants—if he was acting out the violence among us. I have tried to write about this. I have tried to write about this.

He took my hand. He said, All this time. Nothing.

I looked into the mirror in the bathroom—no one stared back. I held my hand out to the empty mirror— the image of nothingness. I stood back—my make-up on the counter fell into the sink.

I picked up my lipstick. I held it up to my mouth—

but I couldn't see my mouth in the mirror. I couldn't feel my mouth. I couldn't find it. It had disappeared.

I dropped the lipstick. It crumbled in the sink.

I couldn't speak. I couldn't shout. I couldn't.

I tried to find my face. But my eyes had disappeared.

I found the fragment of lipstick broken at the stem.

What I wanted to say. What I couldn't articulate. The language elusive.

I held my hand out to the mirror, holding on to that fragment of lipstick—of what I wanted to say to this emptiness—the vacant mirror. The reflected nothingness. Of what I wanted to write. I held the fragment of lipstick up to the mirror.

What does violence mean? Where does the word come from? How do you try to describe an act that cannot be put into words? What does it describe? Does the word show a thing? Show a moment? Show an experience of life? Does the word fall short? Does it fail to convey with accuracy a moment in time? The forbidden idea? What is experience with the knowledge of violence as only an approximation?

I began to write the words. I wanted to understand. My mother's face appeared from behind the first few words I had scrawled, but my hand trembled, the lipstick falling again into the sink. I looked up. My mother's image disappearing, fading. The vague outline of mouth and eyes. Was it her image? Was it mine?

I don't know what happened next. My body was not my body. My image was no longer mine. I felt myself falling.

The sleep I slept—perhaps a sleep of escape. From memory? From violence? From the Nazis at the door? From violence against my mother? From the image I could no longer find?

I woke up on the cold tile bathroom floor. I thought I was going to be sick. I pulled myself up, held on to the sink. My mother was there again, in the mirror.

A knock on the door. I had no sense of how long I had slept. The knock on the door again. Perhaps it was morning. Housekeeping. I had no sense of time. A third knock.

When I opened the door there were three men in Nazi uniforms, two from the Kristallnacht of last night, from the bonfire. The third was Luca.

Come with us, one of the men said.

I struggled. To no avail. Their physical power was too great. I couldn't escape. Luca stood in the doorway watching the two men as they tried to drag me out the door. I craned my head back to see into the bathroom. Please don't, I yelled. Please don't. I saw my mother. I said, A mistake. I turned toward them. I'm not a soldier. How could I know? Please, I said. She's done nothing.

Please, I yelled. Please. One man held me as the other man entered the room walking toward the bathroom to get her. Luca looked on. His face empty—absent of expression.

I don't remember falling asleep. When I woke the curtains were drawn—early morning light filtered through blue gauze. I could not remember how or when or what had happened in-between. The night or nights that had followed since I had fallen asleep. I tried to remember the details. All around me—silence.

I turned over in bed—naked beneath the sheets. Beneath the rough blanket. It was difficult to sit up. My neck ached. My face felt hot. I touched my eyes. My make-up had all but been erased. How many hours had I slept? How many days?

When I was a child, my mother used to read and re-read to me the story of *Rip Van Winkle*. I was always amazed at how a man could have slept through a war, waking one hundred years later to discover that the world had changed around him. Those nights—reading together—neither my mother nor I could sleep. Each night—it seemed as if this were our secret—our desire—to find a way to dream.

I reached over to the nightstand. There was still a small bit of water left in the glass. I took a sip. And then another. Until there was nothing left.

I sat up on the edge of the bed. I found my terrycloth robe on the chair—put it on. The fabric hanging loosely on my body.

The room seemed unchanged. Untouched. The diary still on the nightstand next to the empty glass.

I opened the windows. Trace signs of smoke lingered in the early air. There was no movement in the streets. I didn't see anyone. I didn't hear anyone. It was already warm. I closed the windows, dressed and went downstairs to the hotel lobby. Still no signs of life. The clerk at the lobby desk was not there. The breakfast room was silent.

I held my purse close as I walked through the center of town. I returned to the central square. It was as though nothing had happened. The windows were shuttered. The flower boxes remained intact. The fountain continued to replenish itself. I stood there for a long time, unsure of where to go, of what to do.

An elderly woman came down the street, pulling a shopping cart. She stopped in front of me. She spoke to me, but I couldn't understand what she said. She repeated herself. I couldn't understand her. She became frustrated. She raised her arms in the air before she moved on.

I sat down on the edge of the stone fountain and waited.

An hour later a woman who worked at the café in the square unlocked the front door and propped it open. A few minutes later another waitress arrived. She stood on the terrace, smoking a cigarette before she threw it on the ground and stepped on it. She looked around, then went inside.

When I entered the café one woman was wiping down the bar, the other wiping the tables. They both looked up at me when I entered. The woman at the bar waved her hands at me. We're not open yet, she said.

I returned to the square—not sure if it was market day. Emeline unlocked the door to her small shop. She saw me when she turned around without acknowledging my presence.

I took the bus from the upper gates to the next village. I returned to 12 rue des Juifs. It was early. The courtyard was empty—just as it had been the last time I was there.

Clouds drifted above. The high walls and narrow passageways restricted much of the view of the sky. The light—a grey cast.

The woman at the Museum of Torture opened the window and gates. She said, May I help you?

I said, Do you remember me? I was here a few days ago.

She smiled. She didn't want to be rude. I'm sorry, she said. I'm sure I do. Just so many tourists during this period.

Of course, I said.

She said, Would you like to purchase a ticket?

I looked inside.

That's the medieval winemaker's house, she said. You enter through the torture museum upstairs. She pointed to the narrow wooden stairs leading to the ramparts. Will you excuse me—I just need to finish setting up. She went inside, returning with the two cardboard figures dressed as medieval characters with their faces cut out. She propped them up in front of the museum—next to the ancient water well.

When she returned to the ticket window, I approached her. I said, Do you remember when we spoke about the old synagogue here?

I'm sorry, Madame, I don't remember.

I said, Do you know anything about this place? The old Jewish ghetto?

She said, We believe it was over there. She pointed to the building next to 12 rue des Juifs. She said, Those buildings would have been replaced. These aren't the same buildings, she said. These are sixteenth century. The old Jewish quarter was destroyed in 1416.

And the families that were here. Did they remain?

Oh no, she said. There were only two families here. Maybe 16 people.

What happened to them?

A pogrom, she said. The locals, she said. The Jews were slaughtered.

Do you know why?

I believe the locals owed them money. They didn't want to pay. We don't know for sure, she said. A few years ago, we had some experts come. This is what they told us. She said, But even so, why would they come back?

Yes, I said. Of course.

She asked if I'd like to visit the museum. She told me the new exhibit had just opened about the Great War. She said, I think it's worth seeing.

Yes, I said. I'd like to see it. I purchased a ticket. She handed me a small folded information sheet.

She pointed me toward the dark wooden stairs leading to the ramparts. I looked up at the shallow steps, broken in parts, leading to a tight, narrow gallery. Below the stairs—dirt and cobwebs.

I climbed a few steps—looked behind me. A shaft of light from the courtyard. But silence. A cat sat on the brick water well in the courtyard, watching me. I held on to the railing until I reached the ramparts. Gunnery openings in the walls revealed the green hills covered in grapevines covered in haze—below, the river running through the valley.

A sign on the wall read: *Sentry-Walk Used by Patrolling Sentries.*

The stone walkway was uneven. I touched the damp cold walls, following the walkway in the direction of the Thieves' Tower until I reached more stairs—leading in two directions.

A red arrow painted on the wall directed me toward the lower level.

The space grew increasingly tight. I bent over, holding on to the wooden beam as I walked down the broken wooden steps into a small room.

In it, a series of torture devices. Along one wall, the strappado. A series of pulls. Across the room an iron contraption with three holes. A plaque on the wall.

I heard footsteps behind me. I turned around. A man holding a clipboard came down the stairs. He said, Are you a Jew?

What? I asked.

He said, Are you a Jew?

I don't know what you mean, I said.

It's very simple, he said. Are you a Jew?

No, I said.

I don't believe you, he replied.

I didn't answer.

He said, Are you a Jew?

I don't know how to answer that, I said.

He said, I saw you by the water well.

Yes, I said, it's in the courtyard.

What were you doing there?

I purchased a ticket for the museum.

You know what I mean.

I don't, I said.

You poisoned it.

What? I said.

You heard me. You poisoned it.

I don't know what you're talking about.

You poisoned it.

I didn't, I said.

I saw you, he said. Others saw you. You took our money.

That's ridiculous, I said. I don't know what you're talking about.

You do, he said. You took our money and then you poisoned our water.

Please, I said.

He said, Come over here.

What?

Come over here, he said. Turn around.

He took my arms and tied my wrists together behind my back with a thick rope.

You'll answer my questions, he said.

But I don't understand.

You will.

He went over to the wheel that held the rope. He turned the wheel, lifting me off the ground. Space shifted. My shoulders cracking.

He said, Are you a Jew?

Please.

He continued to turn the wheel until I was suspended above the ground. The space around me shrinking. The stone walls. The damp room. I hung by my wrists. My shoulders dislocating.

He said, You need to answer me.

I can't, I said.

Why not? He turned the wheel.

I don't know what you're asking me.

You do, he said. You poisoned our water. You stole our money.

I didn't, I answered. I didn't.

He reversed the wheel, dropping me near the ground.

Please, I said.

He returned to face me. He stood in front of me. He said, You'll answer my question.

I can't, I said.

No?

He went back to the wheel, pulling me upwards off the ground until I hung suspended from my wrists. My shoulders breaking.

He said, You'll confess.

But I didn't do it.

You'll confess.

But I can't.

Confess. You're a Jew.

He turned the wheel, the pain growing increasingly intense.

What have I done?

You're a Jew, he said.

Please.

My limbs were numb. I had no feeling left.

I said, Is that a crime?

He said, It doesn't matter.

What have I done?

It doesn't matter.

Please, I said.

It won't matter.

But I can't move.

Then confess.

To what?

He reversed the wheel, the rope lagging, he dropped me toward the ground.

Would you rather die in pain than confess?

To what? I repeated.

To the question, he said.

What question?

Are you a Jew?

What does that matter?

Because you poisoned our water well. You stole our money.

But I didn't, I said.

Others saw you, he said.

Impossible, I said. I didn't do it.

Did you forget?

What?

You heard me. Did you forget?

What?

Did you forget what you did?

Please, I said.

He turned the wheel again, raising me off the ground.

Why does it matter to you? I said.

Because you're a Jew.

I couldn't feel. I could no longer speak.

Answer me, he said.

I couldn't.

Why aren't you speaking? he said.

I couldn't answer.

Should I take your silence as a confession?

I tried to speak. But I couldn't.

Okay then, he said.

He went over to the trap door below me. He unlocked it. Opened the door. He said, Since you can't remember, I'll release you. I'll release you to the oubliette.

Please, I said.

He returned to the wheel, lowering me to the ground. He untied my wrists. He said, Maybe now you'll remember. He threw me down into the space below.

All around me darkness. Cold. Stone. Night.

I couldn't sit. I couldn't see. When I lifted my arms I touched cold stone. Something ran across my feet. Crawled along my leg. A rat squealed.

I wandered out into a cemetery, crossing gravestones. The grass was damp. Two boys sat in front of a grave. They were silent. They didn't notice me when I passed them.

A wild dog approached. Stood in front of me. I was afraid to move. I stood still. I couldn't move. It ran off.

I looked for my mother's grave. Where was I? All around me grass and stones. Though the cemetery seemed familiar, I wasn't sure I had come to the right place.

In the center of the cemetery, there was a machine.

I checked my pockets to make sure I had money. I had a few coins. Behind me the two boys remained silent, sitting in front of the grave.

I wove my way around the gravestones until I reached the machine. There were instructions. I deposited the first of my coins.

I punched in the name of my mother. I waited. A horse ran up and stopped beside me. It stood there next to me before running off to the far side of the cemetery.

The machine couldn't find her. It asked me for her birthdate. The date of her death.

I punched in those dates.

Time was running out. I had to deposit another coin in the machine.

A bison, or buffalo, now stood next to me.

Please, I said. Please deliver me her history. Why isn't this machine working? I looked around, but there was no one there. No one to hear me.

I deposited my last coin. Punched my name into the machine. Was it not working? It had to work. It had to release the histories of all who were buried here.

Nothing happened. All was silent. The graveyard empty except for the two boys who sat silently before a grave.

Suddenly there were sounds. Footsteps. People approaching. Crowds walking through the cemetery, moving toward me. I wanted to run, to escape. Leave the graveyard. But I couldn't move.

The door opened. A man entered the room. He said, Come with me.

He took me from the small cell up two flights of stairs to a room above ground. There was light. A high window looked out over the countryside. Another man sat at a desk with a logbook. He followed the lines down to the middle of the log, then made a check mark next to an entry.

He looked up from his desk. He said, You're free to go.

Thank you, I said.

He pointed toward me, pointed to my wrists.

I turned my wrists over.

Guard, the man shouted. See her to the next room. He looked away from me, returning to his logbook.

I followed the guard down two flights of stairs. He pointed ahead. He waited, watching me enter the next room before he turned around.

I walked down another flight of wooden steps into a narrow gallery. High walls—on both sides. Reinforced. Dug into the earth. The path buried. Inside the trench. Sandbags lined the walls.

At first, silence. Then, flashing lights. Artillery. Gunfire. Shadows. The path jagged. I turned the corner. I held my hands up to cover my eyes. The gunfire stopped.

In the distance—light. I walked toward the open window that looked out over the courtyard.

Two children—girls—played in front of the water well. They held what looked like dolls. A woman leaned out of the window across the way at 12 rue des Juifs. She called out to the children, Lunch is ready. Come in. Come in. Two boys—teenagers—carrying books, walked together through the courtyard. They stopped in front of the two girls playing by the water well. The girls laughed. I could not hear what the boys said to them. Together they walked toward the door at 12 rue des Juifs. One of the young boys opened the front door. The two girls ran through the door—up the stairs—ahead of them.

I took the bus back to the village where I stayed. It was a short bus ride and I finally began to have a sense of where I was. Despite the circularity of the landscape, the landmarks were now familiar. The road, weaving through vineyards, along farmland, became the landscape that I now lived in. I anticipated each turn the bus driver took. The road signs pointing to places I believed I knew. I believed I understood. How could I leave this place? I knew my grandfather had been here. The book I wanted to write about him. Whose story would I now tell? His story would be lost.

The bus driver stopped at the upper gates by the park and the ancient lime tree. The elderly men sat on a bench in front of the lime tree as they always did— playing chess, bickering loudly. They didn't seem to notice me when I walked past.

I returned to Emeline's shop. It was almost noon. I had hoped they might still be open.

May I help you, a man said.

Is Emeline here?

She'll be back this afternoon.

I'll return, I said.

We'll be closing soon. If you'd like to try some of our preserves, I can give you samples.

That's okay, I said. I can return. I've tried your preserves. And they are wonderful.

Do you want me to leave a message for Emeline? the man said.

I said, Emeline told me she'd speak to her husband about a woman I'm looking for, a woman whom I believe lives here—or somewhere near this village.

I'm her husband, the man said.

I said, Emeline has been so kind. I put out my hand to shake his, but he didn't respond. I said, Emeline told me that you might have known this woman. Her name is Brissac. Perhaps you know her? I believe she'd be quite old now.

He stepped back a bit. Looked up at the ceiling. He put his hands in his pockets. He said, No. I'm sorry. I don't believe so. The name is not familiar.

Okay, I said. I thought she had to have lived here. I was certain of it.

Madame, I know most of the people of this village. My family has lived here for generations. I don't know that name, he said. Is it Jewish?

I nodded.

Madame, no one is left.

I found Luca in the synagogue. He was working on the exhibit. Inès was in the corner, sitting at a table, taking notes.

In the few days since I had seen it, the synagogue had been transformed into an other-worldly space—a fantastical aviary. The sculptures from his studio were now installed. The figure of the woman on her back. The peacock with the serpent's tail hovered near her. Bird-like masks lined the walls. His wall of birds now translated into the guise of bird-men. His Pulcinellas.

Luca didn't look up when I came in. Inès seemed too engrossed in her work to notice. I began to feel claustrophobic, even paranoid. As though ordinary life continued. And it continued without me in it. What happened last night? What I saw, what I experienced seemed now independent of the people around me.

Luca stood next to the figure of the wolf's face with the gaping mouth—the same figure that I had photographed him in.

Luca, I said.

He looked up. He took his glasses off.

The exhibit, I said. It's almost complete?

Yes, he said. Almost done. The opening is tomorrow. Would you like to come?

I held my purse closer. I didn't understand his response. How was I to take it? As if he didn't know me. As if he didn't recognize me. It couldn't be.

Inès got up from her desk, walked past me without saying anything. She asked Luca if he wanted to take a break.

He told her he didn't have time.

She said she'd get them sandwiches from the bakery. When she left, Luca said, She doesn't understand work. She thinks you can take breaks. We have an opening tomorrow.

Yes, I said. I imagine it is difficult to take a break before something like this. I said, The exhibit looks wonderful. These pieces—inside this space. So unexpected. Startling almost.

So you understand it. I'm so glad. I'd hoped to take advantage of the light and space to show my work. One and the same. We can't separate that out, he said. He turned. Standing in front of the sculpture of the giant wolf's head, he put on his glasses.

I told him that I'd hope to see him later.

He turned back around. Yes. I do hope you'll come back for the opening.

I returned to the hotel. I couldn't breathe in the stifling heat. My few belongings were scattered across the room. A mess that I'd have to clean up. I went downstairs and told the woman at the desk that I needed to leave the hotel earlier than I had thought.

She said, That's fine. We'll only charge you for a half-day. Can you tell me what time you'll be leaving? We need to notify housekeeping.

I'll be back to pack, I said, after lunch.

I couldn't face the room. I felt weak. I needed to eat. I went down to the café in the square. I sat down outside. I had a salad and a glass of wine.

I walked through the streets, marking each step, each cobblestone. The facades, the street names. I didn't want to forget anything. I took notes. I drew a map of the village. I entered the street names, the numbers on the houses. I made note of cafes and restaurants and the hotel that I stayed at. I made a note of the synagogue and of Luca's studio. I marked the bakeries and Emeline's confiture shop. The water fountain in the central square. I made notes of the colors of the houses. The shapes of the rooflines. The number of cars parked along the street. My memory would fade. Even this, even this experience would fade. It could all soon be gone.

I returned to the museum. To see the Altarpiece. The guard took my ticket. Pointed to his watch. He said, We'll close in an hour.

I passed through the courtyard under the linden trees, entering the corridor that led to the chapel. Take privilege in the ability to see, in the ability to be here now—in this place—to see what I've seen, to see what I've not seen. Perhaps all sight is absent of foresight? Though I didn't want to believe that.

The crowds were thinning—a few tourists lingered.

Luca had told me how the Altarpiece was moved throughout history, through wars. Passed back and forth—each movement of the Altarpiece claiming its power. It belonged to no one. Could any piece of art belong to someone? he said. He told me that even his own art lacked ownership.

What drew me to this image? This image so far from my being—or was it? Why does the church ask us to understand suffering in relation to the body of Christ? What notion separates us from the body the artist painted?

I found myself drawn to that which I didn't want to see. The image seemed at once real—at once a fiction. How do we escape the horror of the tortured body—decaying? The body failing and falling in the face of what it's asked to tolerate. As much as I wanted to leave this room, I couldn't. The image before me as mysterious and confusing as the moments before I had arrived here. The space I had entered—the space I found myself lost in.

Was there some aspect of sentimentality in this image—or was it an attempt to paint the reality of pain? The body is only a body. Do we ask too much of it?

Painted to heal the sick. Would anyone dying of this disease take solace in this image?

How little I knew of the body. What it feels is the extent to which I grant its being. To stand there was to recognize that what I feel is only what I can know. That vision is the failure to act. That my action is the failure of vision. What I didn't know—to return to that past—to change what I did or what I did not do. Had fear kept me from action?

What is the body? The artist immersed in it. Had this pain been foreign to him? Had he studied that death present around him—describing the dreams that haunted him? What you didn't know when. Was it there—has it always been there—waiting?

The guard came over to me. He said, We'll be closing soon.

What was missing? The gap in the night—undetermined. Repulsed and drawn to the empty darkness which surrounded the moment. I could no longer contemplate this image. Contemplation kept me from action. The image could not avoid the questions I wanted to avoid. Emptiness. So much emptiness—persistent, unforgiving. I looked down at my hands, at my arms, at my feet—watching as each part of me slowly disappeared.

I returned to the hotel. I gathered my belongings. I opened the drawer of the desk. I took out the card that Iris Bloch had given me the first night in the bar of the hotel.

2.

I had the strange sense as I re-read through my writings of the time that the story I had told was true. I cannot say that there was once a before—that I once existed as another.

The woman opened the gates. May I help you with your bag? she asked.

I'm fine, I answered.

Of course. She motioned for me to follow her.

It had just rained. I pulled my case across the wet gravel courtyard to the front door, passing a trellised garden on the left—to the right, a patio that looked out over the sea. It was still light. The violet sky blended into the mountain and the sea below us. She opened the glass entrance door. Please, she said.

The entrance was light, airy. The windows open. The orange curtains billowing in the evening breeze. There was a bar, a few tables. A man sat alone, reading a book, sipping a tea. He did not look up when I entered.

The woman asked for my passport.

I looked down at my purse, opened it. I looked up at her. I could not read her expression. I took it out from an inside compartment.

She held out her hand. I can give this back to you after dinner. You'll have to leave it with me. She took out a logbook from a drawer in the desk.

She said, Have you been here before? You look familiar.

No, I said. I looked around the room. I glanced back at the desk with my passport on it. The day I left the village in the north, I held on to it as though it were now the last thing I owned.

Now, here, I began to wonder if it were all a dream, or this here, that feeling of reliving a moment in time that I had experienced in a previous life. Was it the same? Would it be? Or was it all an illusion?

She said, We serve dinner every night from 6:00 on. She looked at her watch. Of course, the chef has now left. I can offer you a cold plate, she said.

I said, I'm sorry, I missed the earlier ferry.

She handed me a large iron key. She said, You have a room off the patio, near the pool. I think you'll be pleased.

She checked the time again. I'll take you to the dining room before we close for the night. Please have something to eat. You can leave your bag here at the desk—with me.

I can take it with me, I said.

Of course not, she said.

She escorted me to the dining room. Opened the doors. It was empty. No guests. The tables cleared. She brought me to a table on the far side of the room—along the wall. This is your table for the remainder of your stay, she said. She went through the double-doors that led to the kitchen, reemerging with a plate she set down before me. Cured meats and cheeses. Sliced melon.

She came back with two bottles of wine—a red and

a white. She said, These are from a local vintner on the island—just past the village. An easy walk from here. The soil is rich here—volcanic. The wine benefits. She poured me a white wine.

I'll take your bag down to the room, she said. She left, closing the double-doors behind her.

I sat alone in an empty room with a plate of cured meat and cheese. A glass of white wine. A basket of bread. The light had changed—the sky grew dark—the room slowly brightening under the artificial light. But I didn't want to eat. I didn't want to drink.

A young man entered from behind the kitchen doors. His shirt was unbuttoned, his sleeves rolled up. He smiled. Pointed to the windows.

Yes, I said. Please.

He went to the high windows across the room, methodically closing each one. He turned, smiling again before he left—returning through the double-doors leading to the kitchen.

I heard voices in the kitchen, mumbled sounds I could not discern. I thought I saw the kitchen door briefly open.

I took a bite of the meat—the salt lingered. A sip of white wine, then a bite of fruit.

The room, my sense of the past—fused with the moment—the light—the fruit—the wine—the emptiness. How much of my life had disappeared? As though each congregant in the life of my imagination had grown old—disappearing from my line of sight. I wanted deeply, deeply to hold on—but realized that—that, in itself, was magic, some form of desperate narrative that could not would not achieve the likeness of that place and time I wanted to reclaim.

After dinner I found my room downstairs at the end of a hallway. It was small—simple—but clean. White stucco walls. Red tile floors. The woman from the front desk had put my bag on top of the bed. I pulled back the curtains and opened the French doors. Outside my room was a private patio with a table and two chairs. From the patio—the same view as in the dining room—the mountain and the sea. Now an outline in the dark. The patio was just a few steps from the pool—the air fragrant with night-blooming flowers.

I went to the bathroom to wash up. One white towel hung from the curtain rod. I looked in the mirror. The same mirror. A different mirror. But the same. The image returned. The distance between me and that image I could not breach. The division of the night. The smell of smoke. The broken glass. The men knocking at my door. Nazis. Luca's hand on me. My mother's face looking back at me. I turned on the water faucet. I let the water run over my hands. I looked back up, looking back at my image. My face was pale. Dark circles under my eyes. I washed my face and turned off the water.

That night I opened my bag. My clothing was rumpled, haphazardly packed. I took out my grandfather's diary. I took out my notebook. I placed them both on the nightstand by the bed. I didn't undress. I told myself I would dream the language of my memory of my desire. I closed my eyes—unable to sleep. Listening for sounds outside my room—in the hallway—on the patio outside my room. But I didn't hear anything. The corridors were silent.

The next morning I opened the shutters—unlocked the French doors. The gardener was outside pulling weeds in the garden.

It was early, still too early. The breakfast room had not yet opened. I turned around. A man in a white shirt wiped down the wood bar in the lobby. He looked up at me briefly, pointed to his watch, then went back to work.

I left the hotel, following the path—past the fig tree—down to the beach. The small island town was empty. In a café across from the shore—a young boy— maybe thirteen—opened yellow umbrellas on the patio.

I asked him if the café was open. He looked back to the kitchen. Raised his hands to suggest, not yet.

I crossed the road to the beach. There was a chill in the morning air. The mountain rose sharply beyond the cove. The water bled into the skyline, haze covering the landscape. I took off my shoes, walking across the cool white sand to the edge of the breaking water. I let my feet sink into the wet sand. I sat down at the water's edge. My body absorbed into the sound of breaking waves. Absorbed into sight and sound and distance from the past of the past that would soon come to be. Had I reached the end of that landscape of unknowing? How much further could I go? At this point—was it only escape?

How much was any landscape a part of me? How much could I understand the self through it—or understand this—this moment—where I had been, where I had come from, where I was now, where I could only understand the mountain and the sea—particular to this place? Was this it? The end? The last stop in this?

A man in a caftan, carrying cloth bags, walked across the sand toward me. He waved, then shouted, Hello.

I turned away from him.

Hello, he shouted.

I looked down at the sand. I closed my eyes.

He came over to me. He set the bags down on the sand next to me. He said, American?

No, I said.

French?

No.

German?

No.

He said, Where are you from?

I don't know, I said.

He laughed, then sat down next to me on the sand. He said, You're here early. I don't expect tourists here so early. I'm usually alone on this stretch of beach. But really, where are you from? he asked.

I laughed. Nowhere, I said. You?

Ha. The south, he said. I come up during the spring and summer. Make enough money, then I can go back home, bring the money back to my family.

So you're away from them much of the year?

He shrugged. What else can I do?

You must miss them.

Of course, he said. But this is life, isn't it?

We sat there for a few minutes in silence. The sky gradually brightening. Boats appeared on the horizon.

Look at what I've got. He picked up one of his tote bags, emptying it on the sand. He lifted out brightly colored scarves—turquoise blues, pinks and purples, coral scarves woven with gold threads. All beautiful. You need one of these for the island. He placed the coral scarf around my neck. Beautiful, isn't it?

I'm not sure, I said. I took it off—handed it back to him.

Or, perhaps, you'd like these. He emptied the other tote bag. Beads, necklaces and bracelets toppled onto the sand. I think you might like this one. He pulled out a bracelet that resembled small white and brown shells. It's nice, isn't it? Yes, he said. I think this is for you. He handed it to me.

Yes, I said. Very nice. But I don't think so.

Or wait, he said. He picked up a necklace, a strand of blue beads. Turquoise, he said. Yes. Better for you.

I picked it up. Lovely, I said.

Try it on.

Oh no.

Why not?

I didn't answer.

You must, he said. He took it from my hands, undid the clasp. I'll put it on you.

That's okay, I said. I can do it.

No, let me put it on you.

Really. I can do it.

Come on, he said, so easy. He stood behind me. He clasped the necklace around my neck. Standing up, he looked at me. You see, he said. Perfect. It fits you.

I don't think so. I'm not sure. I'm not sure I can afford it.

It's not much, he said.

Still, I answered.

Okay, I see. He began gathering up the scarves and beads from the sand. He said, Don't worry. When you have money, you can pay me. He held out his hand to me.

I can't, I said. I may not see you again.

Of course you will. I'm here every day.

Okay, I said.

It will protect you. It will bring you luck and calm, he said. I will see you again. He picked up his bags. He said, I can see it in your face. It's okay to cry. Then he left, walking down the wet sand along the shore.

I followed the path from the beach that wove along the rocky coastline. The path rose steeply—through the morning haze the vague outline of boats barely visible in the distance. A fruit-seller standing in front of a small cart on the side of the road signaled that the town was just ahead. He held out a bag of cherry tomatoes to me. I told him that I would stop by later—when I returned. He insisted I take one. I backed away. He grabbed my hand, placing a few small tomatoes in it.

The narrow road wound between the green mountain on one side and the cliff and sea below. Cars and scooters sped past. The morning grew increasingly hot. I took off my sweater, tied it around my neck and leaned against the concrete sea wall. The tomatoes were sweet, unpredictably sweet.

On the far side of the road—next to the mountain—a man stood with a movie camera. He appeared motionless—holding the camera—filming the cars speeding past us—between us. At a certain point he noticed me watching him—waved to me from the other side of the road. I turned away and continued walking uphill.

At the top of the hill a promontory—on it, a small white church—stunning in its contrast to the open blue sky and sea. I climbed the steps. From there a cobblestone path led to a Byzantine-tiled archway that formed the entrance to the wooden front door. There was no one around. The sea breaking against the rocks below.

I looked behind me. Unsure if I should go in. Not sure if I wanted to. Luca's face. The Altarpiece. A white pelican crossed the sky then dove to the water. I twisted the iron knob. It didn't open. When I turned around Luca's face was no longer there. The church courtyard was empty. I climbed the steps to the far side of the church that overlooked the sea, the jetty, the harbor.

I returned to the path down to the main village road. Baskets of flowers hung from the light posts. The shops along the road were opening. In the main square, a few men gathered at a café table under a sprawling ash tree.

I turned left down one of the small streets off the main road. I passed a spice shop on the right. Herbs and peppers hung from the striped awning. In front a woman filled a stand with packages of dried herbs. Across the street there was a book shop with a newsstand outside and a stationery shop next door. A little further on was a small shop with a sign that read: *Cartographer's Notebook*. I entered through the beaded curtains.

Inside the shop was crowded with maps and books and globes. Images of defined and redefined landscapes surrounded me. I touched the turquoise beads that hung around my neck. A woman sitting at a desk looked up—asked if she could help me.

Just browsing, I said.

She nodded, then looked back down at the notebook in front of her.

There were tables filled with boxes, pamphlets and charts. On one table a small box filled with old prints—in no particular order. I looked over at the woman. She didn't look up. I flipped through the prints. Images of what seemed to be the island, of a group of islands. In another print—a woman carried a jug of water down a narrow cobblestone street. There were drawings of birds, flowers, trees—native—exotic. At the bottom of each drawing a name—in what appeared to be Latin—referencing the species.

The bookshelves contained worlds named and renamed—maps of this and the surrounding islands: topographic, street, road maps, land shifts, the sea floor. The volcano, the towns, the restaurants, the cafes, archeological sites. Shifting images—images from early drawings of the islands and landmasses, the sky—a map of the stars. How to make sense of these landscapes of these spaces that needed to be contained to be understood in relation to each other? Historically, socially, politically, environmentally? The shifting landscapes of time and space and memory. How to understand them within the context of where I was here and now.

I pulled a book out of the shelf. Many of its pages were blank—scattered throughout, images of the island—drawings—the volcano, an inlet, the castle—a jetty—gardens. Tucked into the back of the book was a separate map of the island that unfolded. The map was just an outline of the island—no landmarks—no signposts. No streets. It reminded me of a book I had when I was a child. I would practice copying images—learning to draw.

I bought the book and the map. The woman at the desk placed a bookmark inside the book, then wrapped the book in brown wrapping paper. She thanked me before handing the package back to me.

I went back to the central square and sat down at a café table under the ash tree. I placed the book and map on the table.

A young woman came out to the table. I ordered a coffee. When she left I noticed that the man with the movie camera sat at a table across the way. He held his camera in front of him, looking through the viewfinder. The woman returned with my coffee. The man noticed me watching him. He smiled. He motioned for me to join him. I held my hand up to suggest that I wouldn't. He smiled.

A few minutes later he stood at my table. May I? he asked.

Okay, I said.

He pulled out the chair across from me and sat down, placing the camera carefully on the table in front of him.

I saw you walking along the beach, he said. Earlier. This morning.

Yes, I said. I've just arrived.

I can tell.

The young woman returned with a cappuccino and brioche. She placed it in front of the man.

Thank you, Maria, he said. He turned back to me. He said, My office. He raised his arm to the landscape around him. And this, he said, the most important café on the island.

I didn't know that.

Yes, he said. Everyone came here in its heyday. Everyone. All of the artists. All of the writers. Directors. Musicians. Everyone.

Do they still come here? I asked.

I do, he said. Take a look at what I've done today. He handed me the camera. He showed me how to operate it. Look through the viewfinder, he said. Images flashed before me: the road along the beach—the cars that passed—one car after another. The cars that passed him on the street—small cars—trucks, carts, scooters. Each image blurring into the next. A mirage of motion of color. He said, Beautiful, isn't it?

Yes.

I've recorded a moment in history, a moment in time. My memory. My landscape. I've been working toward this my whole life. This will be a great film, he said.

I can see that, I answered.

Eliade, he said. He held out his hand to shake mine.

I shook his hand. I felt his age. The wrinkles. The dry quality of age. Yet his eyes betrayed that age.

He said, Are you an actress?

No. Why?

I just imagined you were. Here you are. On this island. At this café.

No, I said.

Maybe you can play a role in my film.

I didn't know where he was going with this. I sat back in my chair.

He said, I've got to work all day today. Let's go to the beach tomorrow.

I'm not sure, I said.

Why not? It's so warm out. It will be warmer tomorrow. I'll come get you tomorrow. Around 1:00. I'll bring my daughter.

Your daughter? I asked.

Yes. I think you'll get on well with her. We have lunch together every Sunday. We'll come get you and we'll have lunch at the beach.

I don't know, I said.

Why not? he insisted.

After a moment I agreed. Okay, I said.

Tell me where you're staying.

At a hotel at the top of a hill looking out over the bay. I gave him the name.

I'll see you tomorrow, he said. He took back his camera and stood up. We'll have a wonderful day at the beach. I'll bring my camera. He held his camera up to his face. He looked through the viewfinder. He positioned it toward me. I covered my face with my hand.

He laughed. Don't worry, he said.

Yes, I answered.

Eliade waved to Maria who stood in the doorway of the cafe. He walked briskly across the pebble courtyard to the main road that led back to the beach.

I don't know why I had agreed. I will never know. Some weakness or fear within me. Some desire to please, some fear of saying no. Was I doomed to repeat the mistakes of the past? To continue to replay the past in the present? Not knowing this man, I had agreed. How different were they—Luca, Eliade? I no longer knew whom to trust. How could I go on without some sense of belief? Some sense of trust. How far I had come to discover I was lost.

After he left I took out the map and the book of the island. I opened the book. I looked through the images—searching for an image of the café. I couldn't find one.

Perhaps Eliade had exaggerated its importance. On the first page I wrote down the name of the café and the address. I drew an image of an ash tree. I noted Maria in the doorway. I tried to imagine this café as a center of art and culture. I didn't know how it fit into the fabric of this island, of my experience here. If it indeed had once been such a place. And of what consequence that would have on my need to remain here.

It was quiet now. The table of men playing cards under the tree. The woman standing in the doorway, waiting. I wasn't ready to take notes. What would I write? What could I write? How could I?

I had looked through the viewfinder on Eliade's camera. What I saw before me—a heightened vision of the landscape he filmed. A heightened vision of an image that so contrasted with the quiet that existed here. I would need time, time to find my bearings, time to discover why I had come here, to discover where I would go.

Three men holding instruments came into the courtyard. They stood on the far side, setting up, getting ready to play. A bass, a cimbalom, an accordion. The man with the cimbalom looked at the other two musicians, smiled, and, at once, an eruption of sound filled the courtyard. Romani jazz. Music that escaped the perimeters of this café, moving rapidly into rhythms of speed, of light, of the movement to summer.

A few children walked past. And suddenly, in the once quiet courtyard, a crowd gathered around the musicians—children, mothers with baby strollers. Shopkeepers in the piazza came out and stood in front of their shops.

I put the book and map in my bag and took out Iris Bloch's business card. When Maria came back I paid the bill and asked her for directions to Iris's address.

I followed Maria's directions. I took a small winding street that broke off from the main artery of the village. The music growing ever-distant. The winding streets narrowing as I approached a steep incline.

At first small shops lined the streets. I stopped in front of a shop that sold electronics, looking at the objects displayed in the window—mostly outdated phones and computers. There was a dry cleaner and a shop with beaded curtains that advertised meat and poultry. There was a sense of time past, of a world that had been left behind.

Past the shops there were apartment buildings—the windows shuttered—each building distinguished by a different color—yellows, whites, pinks. Though each building distinguished by another color, the colors differed from the villages that I had left behind in the north. The colors—muted, bleached, echoing the sun and the sea, the salt air. Clothing and towels hung from clotheslines on the apartment balconies.

I followed the steep incline until I found 36 via Léal.

There was a number above the lintel. Other than that not much distinguished this building from those around it. I had imagined I would find a shop—or a sign listing the business. There was nothing. I rang the doorbell.

It was lunchtime. Everyone was inside eating, avoiding the heat. Sounds emanated from the closed apartment buildings—dishes clanking, children laughing.

No one answered. I rang again. I checked the business card. I knocked on the door. No answer.

I stopped an older woman walking up the street, carrying two bags of groceries. I showed her the card. She put her bags down on the sidewalk. Took the card. Put on her glasses.

Oh yes, she said. She pointed to the building in front of us. Here, she said.

Do you know her? I asked.

Yes. Yes. This is right. She lives here. She travels a lot. I don't think she's here now. I haven't seen her lately.

Do you know when she might return?

She'll be back. She always returns.

She picked up her bags. Opened the first one to reveal garlic, onions, celery, tomatoes. She opened the other. Inside—a rabbit—still alive. Tomorrow's lunch, she said. And laughed. A wonderful Sunday lunch. She closed the bag. She said, Check back again. She'll return. She continued up the street, unlocking the door in the next building—disappearing inside.

I leaned against the building, feeling the cold stone beneath the pink stucco walls.

Iris had to exist. She would return. I hoped for that. With the growing heat, I began to doubt myself. I began to doubt my decision to come here. I didn't know her. I didn't know anything about her. I didn't know Luca. I didn't know Eliade. I didn't know where I was. I don't know how long I leaned against the stone wall. I didn't know where to turn next. Marking time, I thought. That's all I'm doing. Marking time. I put away the business card that Iris had given me.

I followed the small winding road up the hill until I could see the sea. A slight breeze broke the heat. I found my way to the coastline and retraced my steps back to the hotel.

I contemplated her name—the name Brissac. I thought that if I contemplated her name long enough I would have some sense of who she was of where she was—of how I would find her.

That afternoon I returned to the hotel, changed into a bathing suit and put on the white terrycloth robe I had found in my closet. I lay in the sun. I floated in the salt-water-thermal pool. I kept my new book next to me. I didn't look at it. I didn't even pick it up.

I didn't speak to the other guests. We exchanged smiles—nods—simple acknowledgments that we were here together without engaging in anything more than that acknowledgment. The sun was strong. Most of the guests in the hotel had devised some method for shifting their movements—for shifting their lounge chairs to accommodate the increasing heat.

There was a large bougainvillea tree on the far side of the pool. Beneath it, two women reclined on lounge chairs, taking turns applying sunscreen on each other's backs. I watched them intently—afraid they would discover that I watched them. I wore sunglasses. They wore sunglasses. Perhaps we were all in disguise.

I fell asleep. I dreamt about a young girl. I was in my mother's house—cleaning, wiping down the wood furniture that had gathered so much dust. When I entered the bathroom I found the girl. She sat on the edge of the tub. She was naked. Emaciated. Her body that of a ten-year-old. Her face was large—much too large for her body. But it was beautiful. She wore make-up, false eyelashes. There were mirrors on the vanity—many mirrors. And it seemed that she had been there—at the vanity—putting on make-up for hours.

Who are you? I asked.

I'm homeless, she said.

Why are you here? What are you doing here?

Please don't tell your mother. I come here sometimes. She doesn't know it. Well, maybe that's not entirely true. Sometimes I think she knows it.

You have to leave, I said. As soon as I said it, I wasn't sure if I should have asked her to leave. She may have needed to stay. Perhaps my mother wouldn't care.

She followed me—out of the bathroom through the bedroom and into the hallway. She didn't put on clothes. It was as though she wandered from home to street naked all of the time—having no sense that this was out of the ordinary. I knew that I would—at some point—need to confront my mother about this.

When I woke up, the two women under the bougainvillea tree were gone. The other guests were gone. The groundskeeper was cleaning the pool. He looked over at me briefly, then resumed cleaning.

I was groggy. A bit disoriented. But I picked up the

book. I wrote down my name. I wrote down Iris Bloch's name. I drew a line connecting the two. With no sense of how they might be connected. Of what life or of what world I sought. Of what world I was trying to create.

The groundskeeper looked over at me again. He pointed to his watch.

I gathered my belongings.

I showered and changed for dinner. I went up to the patio where guests gathered for aperitifs. I sat down at the last empty table. I ordered a white wine.

A couple sitting at the next table raised their glasses. Welcome, they said.

I raised my glass in return.

The man said, Your first night here?

I arrived late last night, I said.

You'll enjoy it, the woman answered. We come here every year.

Beautiful, I answered.

Here for long? she asked.

Not sure, I said. We'll see.

I was seated at my assigned table. It looked out over the mountain and cove.

The waiter came to my table with a wine trolley. He suggested a local white that would pair well with the fish for the night.

The couple I had met earlier in the evening sat in the

corner by one of the open windows. The woman waved to me. She came over to me. She said, Please join us for drinks after dinner. We'll be on the terrace. It's so lovely out there. The evenings. I do hope you'll join us. If you don't have plans, she said.

Thank you, I said. I will.

Wonderful, she said. I recommend the fish tonight. Local. Beautifully cooked. We'll talk more after dinner.

She returned to her table where she resumed her discussion with her husband.

The room was full now. The guests busy eating and talking. The waiters moving around the tables at a furious yet calculated pace. The spring evening light penetrating the essence of pleasure—those moments as a child when I would stay out in the garden until late into the night, lying on the grass, reading a book, imagining that darkness would never arrive. I had the sense in this moment that the world goes on and I am absent in it.

We had drinks on the terrace. Lemon liquor—a specialty of the island. The night grew increasingly balmy. The waiters closed the umbrellas. As the sun set the mountain beyond the cove faded to an outline.

Aaron and Helen told me that they planned to rent a private boat—to visit a neighboring island. Would I join them?

I told them I had plans for lunch. I was disappointed.

Helen said, We often rent boats—explore the local waters—the coves—the neighboring islands. If not tomorrow, don't worry. We'll do it again, she said.

The night drifted. The winds picked up. The terrace floating above the sea. Aaron said, A hot wind from the south. This time of year.

Helen said, How did you find this place? Not many tourists know about it.

I said, I've been traveling. I wanted to write a book. I'm not sure anymore. Not sure about the book—if I can write it. Not even sure if it means anything anymore. A woman I met in a hotel suggested I come here.

Where are you from? she asked. Your accent—not quite American.

Yes, I said. I'm often told that.

British? she asked. Then hesitated. No. I don't think so, she added.

Aaron interrupted his wife. He said, Helen, let her be.

That's okay, I said. I've been traveling for so long.

Helen looked over at Aaron, then turned back to me. She said, It's isolated here. Quiet. You feel distant from the world, distant from what's happening, the terrible things that are happening now.

Terrible things? I asked.

Oh, she said. Nothing. Just. Well, everything changes.

I said, Do you mean at home? Where you're from. Some danger?

I'm not sure, she said. There's always a threat, isn't there? Even here, she said.

I don't know, I said. Not sure, at times, where I'm at. Where I'm from. I thought that this was all over. Now, I don't know.

Tell me about your home, she said.

Not much to tell, I said.

Aaron said, Please, Helen.

Why can't we talk about this? she said.

Aaron said, Don't worry. She's always nervous, even here. He looked out over the bay. Just look at this, he said. Paradise.

Helen looked down. Picked up her glass of lemon liqueur. How long? Helen asked. How long do you plan to stay here?

I said, I don't know. I've lost track of time. I laughed.

That happens, Aaron said.

Helen said, Once we spent six days crossing the Atlantic. It was a strange trip. Calm and stressful. And suddenly, time became both ever-present and inconsequential. Until, we, too, lost track of time. Each day we lost an hour as we crossed the ocean eastward.

Aaron said, I wanted to write a story about that.

About losing an hour each day. But I'm not a writer. Better to leave it to someone else.

Images of my grandfather's drawings of the ship emerged before me. I saw that ocean crossing. With him on it. Aaron and Helen on a different boat—a different journey—but the same loss of time.

Aaron said, Bad weather during the crossing. We could only see twenty miles in the distance—fog lay on the ocean's surface.

But beautiful, Helen interrupted. Wasn't it? It seemed as though we were free.

Aaron agreed. I could see the strain on his face. Then on hers.

He said, One day at breakfast we met a man who told us about his late wife. How, after his wife died, he traveled the world—always by boat. One boat after another. The more he talked about his wife, the more he told us only about himself. Later, in the quiet of our cabin, independent of each other, we imagined his life, what he did for a living, the son, the navigation, the circumference of the world. He explained his travel as this—the way you hold a rubber band, let it go, and the shortest distance is the circle which you travel. The great circle of time.

I said, I can imagine. But realized that I couldn't. All made up. All an illusion of knowing.

Six days at sea, Aaron said. The silence. The sound

of the water. By the end of the trip, we no longer needed to speak.

Helen said, We listened to the sea—to the water. It's not as bad as it sounds.

Aaron looked over at his wife. He said, We're here now. He looked at me. He said, Now that we're here we no longer care. Every year, he said.

When I returned to my room, I imagined their life. Their six days crossing an ocean. From the side of the ship I watched with them as they moved across distance. Each day at noon receiving readings of their position, moving further away from and further to— calculating time as repetition as movement displaced perspective. The navigation. The circumference of the world. The way you hold a rubber band, let it go, and the shortest distance is the circle which you travel. The great circle of time.

That night in bed I heard the water as it washed against the ship. For six nights I would hear that sound.

As the ship moved, it displaced the water. By the fifth night, no one spoke.

Had they met? On the river—in a boat heading north along the Rhine? Or at the port in Rotterdam? Joseph—thirteen? He traveled with his older sister. Was it there he met Brissac? His name? Brissac's first name?

A group of boys stood at the stern of the open boat.

Joseph wanted to join them. He asked his sister Dora. They weren't supposed to part. She was there to take care of him. Every step. From their village, by foot, to the boat along the Danube. To the boat along the Rhine. From there they would depart. Leave by ship from Rotterdam.

1907. Romania. The Peasants' Uprising. They blamed the Jews.

Dora told him, Yes. He could leave, go. She was young. Too young. Only sixteen.

He ran off. Was always running off. Getting into fights. Running away. From home.

Dora watched him as he ran off to join the boys at the stern.

This is where he met Brissac. Brissac was older—by a few years.

He'd said, Just call me Brissac. That's how you'll remember me.

Joseph did.

They spoke the same language—a version of the same language. Joseph would later forget it. Most of it. Forget Yiddish. He'd wanted to forget it.

Brissac said, Look what I found. He took a small round object from his pocket. He handed it to Joseph.

What is it? Joseph asked.

A compass, Brissac said. You've never seen one?

Joseph shook his head.

This way we make sure the boat goes in the right direction. Brissac took back the object, held it up, finding direct north. You see, he said. Watch the needle. We're heading north.

Where did you get it? Joseph asked.

A man on the boat gave it to me. When I got on. In Strasbourg.

Who?

Just some man on the boat. I traded it.

For what?

A pen, he said.

Can I get one?

I don't know, he said.

I'll try.

Okay, Brissac said. If you can't find one, I'll give you mine. I'll trade you for something else.

You don't need it?

If I give you mine, you can take over. You'll be the navigator.

Joseph smiled. He hardly ever smiled. He looked back across the boat at his sister Dora. Dora leaned against the railing. She had her eyes closed. It was a warm day. Mid-summer. The sun beat down. The open-air boat seemed still—but it wasn't. It moved, lumbering down the river through a green landscape, hillsides dotted with villages. Steep cliffs. Broken stone castles in the distance.

But I don't have anything, Joseph said.

You must have something.

I don't know. I don't think so.

See if you can find something, Brissac said.

Joseph ran back across the boat to Dora, who stood still against the railing with her eyes closed in the mid-day sun. He said, Dora, do you have anything, anything I can trade for a compass?

Dora said, What? We can't trade anything. We don't have anything.

Please, Joseph said. I need to find something.

I don't know, she answered. She looked inside her bag. I don't know, she said.

Joseph ran off. He wandered the open-air boat. He came across a man sitting on a chair on the deck. The man held a book in one hand—a pipe in the other. He went up to the man. Joseph said, Can I trade you for something?

The man smiled. He said, What do you have to trade?

Joseph looked around him. He didn't know what to say.

The man said, I only have a book and a pipe.

Joseph dug inside his pockets. He had nothing.

The man said, Are you sure you don't have anything?

I don't know, Joseph said. I must have something.

The man said, I'll give you my book. I've finished reading it. You can have it. A gift. The man handed Joseph the book. It was a small book. Joseph looked at the cover. He couldn't read it. The language seemed familiar yet foreign.

The man said, It's a good book. I think you'll enjoy it.

Joseph stood still in front of the man, holding the book.

The man said, Don't worry. You'll read it someday.

Joseph ran off. He ran back to Brissac. He held up the book. Look what I found, he said.

Brissac smiled. He said, Okay then.

They got off the boat in Rotterdam. They waited in immigration. Waited for their boarding passes to be stamped. Waited for the ship, the Potsdam. They waited there together. For hours. For days. For weeks. We waited there together.

Brissac didn't get on. They didn't stamp his pass.

Joseph, I said. He stood in front of me, holding the

compass in his hand. Joseph, I said again. He looked up, looking past me. And I thought he heard me calling him. He didn't. He didn't hear me. He didn't respond.

Eliade arrived at the hotel at noon. I found him standing near the entrance, leaning on the registration desk.

Ready? he asked.

Luisa was at the desk. She looked over at me, then returned to the logbook in front of her.

Come on. My daughter's waiting for us.

I handed Luisa my room key. She placed it on the board hanging on the wall behind her.

We walked across the gravel path through the open gates to his car. The day had grown increasingly humid—but the sky still clear. He pointed to the sea. We'll go to the beach after lunch, he said.

We drove down the road that led to the beach—then made a sharp turn to the left, leaving behind the cove, heading inland. He said, My daughter's visiting an old friend on the other side of the island.

Eliade drove with one hand on the wheel. He turned on the radio. Listen to jazz? he asked. He looked over at me, then looked out of his side window. No one cares anymore, he said. No one cares.

We passed waterfalls—small villages. Dense green foliage. I rolled down my window. Leaves and branches brushed against the side of the car.

One of my favorites, he said, pointing to the stereo.

Listen to that saxophone. I knew these guys, he said. Years ago. Remember the jam sessions? Different in those days. Don't you think?

I don't remember, I said.

Really?

I didn't know how to respond.

Degenerate music, he said. Ha! What were they talking about? But it came back. Came back stronger than ever. You don't remember the clubs? The late-night jam sessions? It's getting claustrophobic here. What do you think? Can't work. Can't work anymore. Not the way I used to.

The road descended—the car swerved. A line-up of cars ahead of us. A bus came barreling down the other side of the narrow road.

I held on to the seat, feeling my hands go numb. I felt sick. I wanted him to slow down. I was afraid to ask.

This island, he said. What choice do I have? My film's almost finished. Then everything will change.

Change? How?

I'll return. Return home. Work like I used to.

Do you want to leave? I asked.

He didn't answer.

You're working here, I said.

He looked straight ahead. He wouldn't respond.

I re-arranged the turquoise beads on my neck. They were still there.

We arrived at the main street that wove through the village—shuttered shops and apartments lined the road. Cars parked on the road, on the sidewalks. The street was quiet—

the time of day. A medieval castle built into a large rock rose above the village.

We walked down a side street to a nondescript apartment building. Eliade rang the buzzer. The door unlocked.

We entered through the vestibule. When we arrived the door to the apartment was open. The man in the doorway introduced himself as Yannis. He shook Eliade's hand. We followed him through a long hallway. The rooms were dark. The shades drawn. The heat, Yannis said. Stifling. Sit down, he said, motioning to couches in the living room.

Where's Lidia? Eliade asked.

In the bedroom. Lying down.

Wine? Yannis asked.

He returned from the kitchen with a bottle of white wine and three glasses. How long have you been here? he asked.

A couple of days, I said.

What do you think?

Beautiful, I said.

I took a sip of wine. It had the same dry mineral

quality of the wine I'd had the first night I had arrived on the island.

Yannis said, What brought you here? How did you meet Eliade?

I didn't want to respond. I turned away.

Eliade pulled out his movie camera. He stood up and walked over to the far wall and began filming the room.

I grew up with his daughter, Yannis said, gesturing toward Eliade. He was famous—in those days.

Meticulously approaching each photograph—each painting on the wall—moving slowly toward each image with a kind of childlike surprise, Eliade seemed not to take notice of Yannis—of me.

When we were young—he always traveled. All over the world. He often came to this island. A filmmaker. Crazy, Yannis said. The life he led. Lidia—she was beautiful then. Quite beautiful. Always at my house. After school. Her parents weren't around. Somehow we all ended up here, he said.

Should we check on her? I asked.

Ah—she'll be fine. Too much to drink. In this heat.

Eliade went into the next room.

Yannis said, Come. See my garden. He led me through the kitchen to a door that led outside, down three steps, leading to an open grassy space. I'm sure you didn't expect this, he said. In the middle of the village. He pointed to the corner. I usually grow a small garden. Tomatoes, peppers, eggplants. Not this year.

Why not?

I'm not sure, he said. I couldn't do it.

We walked out onto the dry grass. Silence around us. I took another sip of wine.

He said, We've all come here from somewhere else. And you? Why here? He pressed me. He said, Really. Tell me.

I said, I've been traveling. For a while. I imagine I needed to find someplace, somewhere, to rest. I'd been traveling the villages on the mainland—following my grandfather's WWI diary. It became too much.

Why? he asked.

I don't know. I started to feel too unknown. Too unknowing in a culture I didn't understand.

Yes, he said. I see. I think I understand. When it's not your home, your language. You miss signals. Maybe I can help you.

I didn't answer him. I was unwilling to commit.

And Eliade? How did you meet him?

In a café in the center of town. He had been filming the road along the beach. He wanted to take me to the beach today. I don't know why I said yes.

You're obviously overly trusting.

I don't think so.

We'll talk, he said. It's almost time for lunch. Can I refill your glass?

We returned inside. We found Eliade in a small room, leafing through a box of old music albums. Eliade sat on the floor, filming each album he took out of the box.

Lidia emerged from the back bedroom—naked.

Yannis said, Maybe you want a robe.

Oh no, she said. Too hot.

She walked through the room to the living room and lay down on the couch. Another glass of wine? she asked.

Yannis poured her another glass. He left the room, returning with a white terrycloth robe. He placed it over her body.

Eliade held an album in his hand. Look, he said. He set it down on the table. Filmed the cover. Then handed it to Yannis.

Lady Day, Eliade said. No one better.

Yes, Yannis added.

I want to hear her.

Now?

Yes.

I said, Are we going to lunch?

Eliade said, Can we listen to Lady?

I took another sip of wine. Eliade sat down in a chair across from the couch.

Yannis got up—put the album on the turntable.

Lady's voice was deep, raw, pained.

Lidia said, Oh please.

Eliade said, Listen to that voice. Listen.

Yannis looked over at me.

Eliade sat down in a chair across from us. He put his face down, covered his eyes with his hands.

Lidia began laughing.

Yannis said, We'd better get some food.

Eliade said, I loved her. I really loved her.

Lidia said, Come on.

I loved her, he said. His body shook. He wiped his eyes. Listen to that voice.

Lidia turned to me. So sentimental.

Yannis stood up.

Eliade turned to me. We've got to go.

But aren't we going to lunch?

We've got to go.

He stood up and came to get me on the couch. He held his hand out to me.

I stood up. Picked up my bag.

Yannis said, We should all go to lunch. He followed us to the front door. I'm not sure you should go with him.

I shrugged.

Really, he said.

I don't know, I said.

Where are you staying? he asked. I'll come see you.

Okay, I said.

He stood in the doorway, watching us.

The heat hit us as soon as we left. My body struggled to respond. Fighting the heat, fighting movement.

We got in the car.

Eliade said, I need to stop at my studio.

Eliade drove back across the island. I regretted having left Yannis's house. I regretted having left the hotel. I thought about the couple I had met the night before. I imagined them in their rented boat—traveling to local islands. Lying in the sun. Swimming in the sea.

Eliade didn't speak. He drove fast. We stopped at a small village. Shops and restaurants—shuttered. He said, We're here. My studio.

From the outside the studio appeared to be another nondescript building. A friend lets me use his office, his studio. He knows I need to finish my film. It has everything I need. I come here every night.

He stopped on the sidewalk in front of the building. He told me that he hoped to find the lost city. In his dream he wandered through ruins—broken city gates, arenas, small rooms painted with faint images of life. He wandered through the dusty ruins—weaving through the broken streets. He wore a white straw hat—the sun beat down—and the more he wandered the more distant he became.

The city sprawled the landscape—reaching to the sea.

The city held his imagination, he said. For it was a city where each inhabitant had spent lifetimes—as we had.

Did they know that in a moment it could be gone? The city broken with the future—the landscape an artifact of consciousness.

He said, there are cities like this below our feet—we stand above them. They will find our city someday.

He unlocked the door to the office building. I followed him inside.

Eliade led me down a carpeted hallway to a small screening room. About thirty chairs.

He said, I know why you're here.

You do?

Of course I know why you're here. The reason everyone is here. He said, Take a seat. Sit anywhere. I'll be in the projection room. I need to show you my film.

I sat down in the middle of the room. I checked my watch. I knew I wouldn't make it back to the hotel for dinner. Eliade turned off the lights. The room was dark but cool. I had gotten myself into this. I had no choice but to see it through to the end.

The screen lowered. The projector started.

The first images—daylight—cars following one after another. I watched the images Eliade had shot the morning before. Along the path from the beach. One car after another. Following each other around the bend. A fruit cart parked across the street. A man—a fruit-seller standing next to the cart. The sea wall just beyond.

The next image—night. The same space—the same place from which to watch the cars—following one another around the bend that led from the beach to the town. This time—in the dark—the images blurred. The lights running into each other. Headlights—backlights. Streaks of color. The sea wall—a blur in the night. The camera steady—moving closer toward the lights—toward the image of the lights fragmented—abstracted—a landscape of color set against a dark field.

The view of the sea from the top of a hill. The camera still.

Then—the beach—the waves. The water. The intense focus on the water washing across the sand. Moving closer to the sand, the dirt, the water. The molecules. Sunlight refracting off of the sand—off of water. Multilayered—the images blurring the particles of sand—close-up—becoming increasingly abstract. The image of sand—now an image of concrete.

The screen turned dark. Ten seconds—fifteen—then—perhaps—a minute. I sat watching a dark screen—waiting.

A painting. Expressionistic. A woman with dark hair—parted on the side—falling on her shoulders. Standing in front of a red doorway—against a blue background. Wearing a purple dress. Her skin—tinged green. Her eyes gazing—off-centered—into the distance. Her expression one of indifference. Perplexing—or perhaps ambivalent. The *Mona Lisa.* The expression you cannot define. The camera moved closer toward the image—closer until all I could see were the woman's dark eyes. Those eyes that eventually gave way to a dark screen.

And then an image—what looked like an image from the war. Black and white—old footage—cutting out—returning. Soldiers. Soldiers in SS uniforms standing on a hill—behind gunnery—looking out at a sea. The same point that I believed I had looked out at yesterday. The cove. The hills surrounding the cove.

A photograph—a photograph of a man—Eliade, perhaps. Younger. Much younger, smiling. Sitting in a café—surrounded by three other men—sitting in a booth. The image moving closer toward him. Toward Eliade. Toward his face—toward his eyes—eventually dissolving.

A sidewalk. Broken pottery. Fragmented shards of blue and green tiles. The shape—the shape of an island. The sea-colored tiles set in concrete. In the center of the shards of tile—words—words that seemed to read: *Artists and Friends of Saint Cecilia.*

The image rested on these words before turning to the image of a car burning on a side street. A narrow street that looked like it was in a medieval village. The flames consumed the car. And then an explosion. The image of the car replaced by the image of a house. A burning house on a quiet street surrounded by other small houses—pine trees—birch trees. Flower pots in window boxes. A different house. Perhaps a house in the north. The flames seen through the windows of the house. The house gradually consumed by flames.

The image of the house replaced by a pile of books on fire in the middle of a square—next to a fountain in a medieval village. The books burned until there was nothing left but soot and ash. Ash drifting into the air. Clouding the image. The street—darkened by smoke.

The smoke gave way to a street lined with broken glass. Shards of glass covered the street, the sidewalk. The image at first taken from a distance—moving ever closer toward the glass—moving toward the glass until it refracted in the light—until it became an abstraction— an image of broken shapes—indistinguishable—in its brokenness—undeniable.

I didn't want to watch anymore. I closed my eyes. I put my hands over my eyes. There was no sound in the studio. No soundtrack that preceded or followed the images. Silence save for the sound of the projector. I heard the images before me. Even with my eyes closed.

Because my eyes were closed. I could hear the sound of what I knew was about to come.

I felt a presence next to me. When I looked up I saw Eliade standing on the side aisle of the theatre—across from where I sat. He held his camera in front of him. He stood still. I don't know how long he had been standing there—standing there watching me—standing there filming me—filming me watching the images that he had shot.

The next morning Luisa knocked on my door. She said, A man is here to see you. Waiting in the lobby.

I dressed and went upstairs. It was Yannis. He said, I've been worried about you. Can we talk?

Yes, I said.

We sat at a small table on the patio. We ordered two café au lait and two waters.

He said, Are you happy here?

Yes, I said.

But it's a hotel. He looked around. He said, Wouldn't you prefer a place of your own? Your own kitchen. A sense of quiet.

I'm happy here, I said. I don't mind impermanence. In fact, I find solace in it.

I don't understand that.

I'm not sure I do either, I said. I don't think I belong anywhere.

That woman who runs this place. Strange, I think. I don't like the way she looks at me.

She's okay, I said. Proprietary. Controlling. It's her place. Besides, I don't know how long I'll be here.

About Eliade, he said.

Yes.

I worried about you. All night. I called this hotel. They said you weren't in.

I got in late. Not what I'd expected. He took me to his studio. Wanted to show me his film. Then he wanted to eat.

He's not well, Yannis said.

Yes, I said.

He was great, he said. At one time. Great. An important filmmaker.

I believe so, I said.

He can't escape. Can't escape the past.

Maybe, I answered.

He's been here a long time. He can't return. You know about him? Why he's here?

No, I said.

He was getting too close. Too close.

Too close to what?

Too close to what's happening. Filming it. The rise of it—again.

Of what?

Fascism, of course.

I don't know, I said. I couldn't shake the images that were before me. The images he had shown me the night before. The images I had experienced.

They burned down his house. He lost everything. His past. His memories. Everything. He had gotten too close.

Lost in them—his memories. Trying to recreate them. Necessary, I think.

Yes, Yannis said. But you need to be careful.

He's quite old. Harmless, I think.

I don't know, Yannis said. He's reckless. His daughter's a mess.

You grew up with her?

She had no sense of home. Both parents gone—affairs. Drugs. She was always in chaos.

So his stories—true?

I believe so, he said.

The waiter came to clear the table.

And you? he asked. You must be here for a reason?

I didn't answer.

Yannis said, Let's go for a walk.

We left the hotel and walked down the steep hill—past the fig tree. He reached up to pull a fig from the tree. He said, Not quite. Another week, I think.

We walked on—down toward the beach.

I said, I don't understand this place.

That makes sense. He stopped at the bottom of the hill. He watched a gecko run up the wall. Amazing, he said. Isn't it?

Yes, I said.

We turned right, following the path away from the cove and along the coast toward the port.

We walked under a bridge then stopped before he turned around. Yannis said, I've lived here for years. Before there were tourists. Before Eliade—before Eliade came with his daughter. He said, I was studying an early settlement. An ancient Greek colony. I believe they were the first here. A center of trade. We found important artifacts—pottery—tools—amphora. Some even believe it was Circe's island.

I laughed. So, we may all be stuck here? Transformed into swine?

That's the theory, he said. Last stop before the underworld. Or we can't go home.

That's why you're here? That's what you do here?

Yes. And no, he said. I don't work much these days.

Why not?

Actually, I'm stuck, he said, laughing. A hearty laugh—a wonderful expression. His expression then changed. Some sense of gravitas took over. He said, I returned home. I knew what was coming. Why I had to leave home and come back here.

The heat grew intense. My body fighting the heat, moving as if I were moving through planes of shifting air.

We walked up a steep hill to a promontory that looked out over the sea—separated by a cove on one side and by a small dock of boats on the other. Children played in the water among the rowboats.

He said, I want to help you.

Okay, I said.

Really, he said. Please leave the hotel. Come stay with me.

Why?

I live alone. Have an extra room.

I don't know, I answered.

Think about it.

I said, I'm not sure I want to stay.

He said, You will, I think. What choice do you have? It's where we've all found ourselves. Isn't it?

I said, Can we move into the shade? Get something to eat?

Of course.

We went to a small restaurant on the beach. We sat on the deck over the sand. We seemed to float there. Within reach of the water.

We got a carafe of white wine. Yannis ordered a plate of small fried fish.

He said, I left my lover. I left him. I had to. My family—his family—didn't understand.

I'm sorry, I said.

No, he said. I tried to change my life. Tried to change who I was. I married a woman. I left Christos behind. I left him behind. And then I left her behind.

Do you speak to them? Ever?

No, he said. That's my failure.

But you can contact them, contact Christos.

I don't think he'd answer me. I don't even know where he is.

I understand, I said. I've made too many mistakes. Well, not sure.

He laughed.

Yesterday I told you that I don't know where to go. I don't know where I belong. I left home.

The waiter brought us a plate of fish.

Yannis said, Eat it all—the head—the bones. He picked up one of the small fish. Reminds me of home, he said.

I said, I told you about my grandfather's diary. How I'd been following it. Eventually it led me to a village in the north. I was looking for someone, a family, at least—anyone who might have been left there. I got caught. A strange sense of violence. Of a violence I saw happening that I felt would start to grow. I couldn't believe it would happen. Not again.

You see that hill over there? He pointed to the hill above the cove. During the war the Nazis took it. Their lookout.

I saw that—in Eliade's film. I'm sure that's what I saw. The Nazi soldiers on the hill.

I have to believe that we're all safe here. That's why you're here, he said. I believe that's why you're here.

I don't know, I said.

Eliade, he said. Be careful. Not because he'll harm you. I'm sure he won't. I just can't trust him. His intentions. I can't quite read him now.

I believe he just wants someone to see him. To see his work. To feel important again. To know that his work is appreciated.

I took one of the small fish. Bit into it. The taste salty, crunchy. Funky. The taste of the sea.

I asked, Are these fresh?

Of course. You've probably never tasted fish right from the sea.

I took a sip of wine. It cut the strange taste I wasn't used to.

Eliade—he lives too much in the past. Can't move forward. Can't understand that what we've got here is what we've got here.

The next course came. A whole fish.

The waiter brought it to the table—then took it back to his station.

The best, Yannis said.

The waiter cut off the head—then the tail. Then cut through the spine. After he filleted the fish, he handed us each a plate—drizzling olive oil over the fish.

It's not bad here, Yannis said.

I couldn't help but feel displaced. I no longer had a sense of home.

As if he understood my thoughts, he smiled. Took a bite of the fish. He said, What do you think?

The fish was delicate. Beautiful. Wonderful.

I knew you'd like it.

I said, I came here to find someone. Someone who offered to help me.

I might know her, he said. It's a small island. Though we often keep to ourselves.

He finished eating. Sat back in his chair. Took out a cigarette. You don't mind?

No. I don't.

He said, I could stay here all day. All day. And into the evening. You don't mind, do you? After, maybe, we can take a walk on the beach—or go into town. He called the waiter over. He ordered an espresso and an anisette.

I miss Christos, he said. I really miss him. He took a sip of his espresso. He began to cry. He said, I had no choice. I knew he wouldn't come here with me. He was afraid. His family couldn't accept him, couldn't accept me. Why couldn't they accept us? When I went to their home for dinner, the sisters would turn away from me. They left the room. Christos would smile—with that inimitable smile—say, forget them. But they couldn't accept him, and, eventually, I couldn't accept myself. There was a feeling growing in the country. I felt it all around me. A resurgence—resurgence of intolerance.

It was everywhere. All around us. It's been happening slowly—so slowly that most aren't even aware of it. Maybe it was always there. That's when I married a woman. She was beautiful. My family accepted her. I believed I was doing the right thing. It didn't last, of course. He said, I know what you felt in that village. Different. But the same. We're different. I had worked on this island. This place. A sanctuary. I needed to go somewhere. He wiped his eyes with his hand. He turned away.

And Eliade? I asked.

Of course, he answered.

And Lidia?

Poor Lidia—she's gone. So gone. At least she's safe here. For now.

The waiter returned with two glasses of anisette. I could see we were not going anywhere. Not at that moment. Not then. We would linger. Linger as a form of movement. I understood. Looking out at the sea. Sipping my anisette. I came to see that wherever I was I longed to be. This was not a form of fear but a form of wanting.

The rock drifted on the surface of the tide. Sponge-like, volcanic. I swam toward the stern of the boat. Sea-wrecked. Soundless. Green black tufa. I collected the rock in my hand. The boat rocked—water lapping. I held on to the boat's ladder.

Yannis held out his hand, helping me into the boat, then handed me a towel. What do you think?

Beautiful, I said. The water is beautiful.

I wrapped the towel around me and sat down on the bench at the back of the boat.

Yannis stretched out on the bench across from me. Closed his eyes. He said, Let me know when you're ready to move on.

One other boat was docked in the cove. Two young boys with snorkels dove into the water. They swam to shore, dug in the sand, entered the caves, then returned to the water.

I took out the map, marking the cove. The rocks. The caves. The sand.

How different this landscape was from the one I had come from. How I wanted to articulate that difference. For that landscape was extraordinary—one of the most exquisite places I had been to.

I didn't know how to begin. How to begin to articulate that difference. The boys swimming in the sea. Yannis napping on the boat. My desire to describe this place. To understand this place in relation to where I had been. Where I had come from. Where I would go. To understand why I had needed to find Madame Brissac. To speak to her. To know why we would all soon find ourselves here. To understand why I had come to this island.

I had made lists of places—the lighthouse, the village, the beach, the boat—the road to the beach which circled the island. I tried to define the landscape—this cove, the caves, the shops. I used these places as signposts, images on a map. I soon came to see that it was the nature of this island that whichever path you took led you back to the beginning—each path a form of circularity. I looked up. From this distance—the island looked like a rock floating.

The sun moved overhead. Yannis pulled up the anchor and started the engine.

We went out into the open sea, passing fishing boats. He looked very happy. Alone—with a sense of abandonment. We didn't speak. But listened to the water—the motor—the water washing across the boat.

He looked back at me as he navigated the rocky coastline. He shouted, We're almost there.

We entered yet another cove. Small boats docked off-shore. He stilled the engine and dropped the anchor.

A young man steering a small motorized boat met us. He held out his hand to me. I held my bag and stepped down into his boat. We docked at the pier, then followed a white sand path to a small restaurant with wooden tables shaded by sun-dried grass umbrellas.

We sat down at one of the long tables. Behind us a family ate and laughed. The waiter brought us a pitcher of white wine with peaches.

Yannis took a sip of wine. Nothing better, he said.

The fruit-sweetened wine—inextricably tied to the landscape. To the sun. The sea. The heat.

You're not happy, he said.

I am.

No. I can tell. You want to return. Go home.

Maybe, I said.

He said, Look around you. He pointed to the sea. What more do you need? You're safe here. Not just safe.

I know.

A young boy—maybe thirteen—brought us toasted bread with chopped tomatoes drizzled with olive oil.

At the table behind us there was a cheer and then applause. And then song.

A birthday, Yannis said.

I turned around. The table—filled with children, parents, grandchildren.

He said, What have you been working on?

I said, I've been marking locations—trying to understand this place.

He said, But what have you been writing?

I said, I'm trying to understand that place I came from—not home—but the home of my grandparents—of my great-grandparents.

And...? What have you found?

I thought about his question. I said, Only the surface. The wars...the violence....the....

The fear? he asked.

The question took me aback, startled me. Yes, I said, the fear. Theirs and mine.

Yannis could see that he'd brought me to the brink of what I hadn't wanted to acknowledge. Reaching over, he put his hand atop mine. He said, I'd like nothing more than to reassure you. It wouldn't be honest. You're courageous, he said.

And I'm a Jew, I said.

And you're a Jew, he agreed. And me? he said.

You might as well be.

Another couple sat down next to us at the table. I took my hand from under Yannis's hand. They greeted us. The waiter brought them a pitcher of wine.

Hungry? Yannis asked.

I don't know, I answered.

He said, If you stay with me you can write. You'll have that space to write. And maybe you'll inspire me. Inspire me to contribute here. To do more. To feel as if I, too, am an artist.

I said, You do contribute here.

He said, Let's go rest—lie down in the lounge chairs. He pointed to the far side of the restaurant—to a covered alcove. A grape arbor. Lemon trees. A sea-grass roof—next to the beach. Maybe after, we'll have something to eat.

I woke half-dreaming on the beach. I watched the woman next to me slowly wake from a sleep where she did not dream—just sounds—the water—the cicadas—the people on the chairs next to her. She woke without dreaming, having felt she had dreamt—sleeping far from the landscape of her knowing.

In the small rock caves just beyond, I imagined seals. A sea life far from ours. Behind us the grape arbor, the lemon trees, the onions strung above. The pale roof-grass.

It was late afternoon. Putting a wrap around herself, the woman followed the white path to the wooden dock where the dockhand helped her into the boat.

I followed him for a long time. I didn't want to make myself known.

When he got off the train in Dover, I stood behind him, the wounded passed him, moving toward the city. He, moving past them. Through them. Nothing left of them. Ghosts moving past us, through us. He marched on through them. At night. Following orders. They, returning from the unspeakable. On trains moving north. He, moving to replace them.

I stood behind him, behind them, wondering how he could keep moving through, moving on. Through the ocean crossing. In the danger zone. The ship ahead of them torpedoed. He had a headache. The storm on the sea. A headache. He got off duty. The sea playing with the ship like a toy, he said. I wanted to put my hand on his head. But he didn't know me. He felt sick.

They left at dark, arrived at 10 o'clock. He spent the cold night in the ruins of Dover Castle. He thought about the ocean crossing, the trainloads of bandaged soldiers. He wrote the name Rose in his diary. All dark, he wrote. Fog and darkness. He slept on the floor of the broken castle ruins.

I shivered in the damp night air, sitting behind him.

In this relic. This broken structure. All around me, men huddled.

He left the next day. Crossed the channel. Arrived in France. He wrote: First instruction in gas.

Another train. A box train. Boxcars. Each car marked: Hommes 40, Chevaux 8. We sat in a train with 40 men. Couldn't move. Couldn't breathe. Then hiked to a small village near the firing line. Hiked all day. Could hardly walk. I tried to keep up. The landscape in ruins. Hollowed out homes. A band of French buglers accompanied us to the next camp.

There were days with nothing to do. Drills. Gas mask drills. Put on the mask. Test it. See if it works. Hike. Learn to shoot with British rifles. Learn to throw grenades. The airplanes overhead. He wrote: Seen a lot of airplanes. The constant sound. Nothing to do. He washed his clothes. Took out his compass. He held his diary. He wrote the name Rose.

It was cold. He slept in a barn. They slept everywhere—in barns, in outhouses, in wine cellars. He wrote: The eats are terrible. Have to think about drills.

The next day the weather cleared. It was nice. He wrote: Got my gas mask. Night again. Slept in a barn.

Had my first bath since Camp Upton.

Always moving. To the next camp. To the next

training. To the next drill at the shooting range. To the next front.

He hiked along the path. I followed him.

A Friday. Full moon. The weather still nice. Hiked with platoon. He wrote: I had the first cup of milk.

A day of rest before the next move. I was so lonely, he wrote. The next day we were to leave for a different town, for Merckeghem, near the line. Hiking again. Moving again. Drill in the morning. Dig in the afternoon.

Trench digging again. Got paid for the month of March. I got drunk as I felt lonesome for Rose.

Trench digging. I had a big head from the night before.

The weather was nicer. I was a little better. & Rose and home and mother.

The first gas attack cloud. Saw a night air filled by gas, by airplanes.

A big hike. The weather was terrible. Drenched by rain. Slept that night in a small room.

The next night he slept on the ground.

I was out digging, he wrote.

I wanted to help him. I didn't know how. How to dig. To keep digging. Through earth and stone. Deeper and deeper into the ground. Into the earth. Buried in it.

June 10: I wrote, Look back at this entry. Cannot read it. Cannot decipher it.

The next day he is back on the train. In a freight car. Slept on the car. 32 boys in the car.

June 18: We stopped in Villoncourt. Temporary. Always temporary. Would move again. Soon. Rain. Constant rain.

A few days later. To Pexonne. Somewhere near the front. The Meurthe River. A few miles from the Alsatian border.

Pexonne. Terrified, he wrote. Near the front.

They told them it was the Quiet Front. Little fighting there. So much time here. Could dig and dig. Dug with the line. In rock. Difficult digging. It was quiet there. So they could take their time. Reinforce the trenches. Solid stone. Reinforced. A barricade of wire. Dug with the line. In rock. Lines of trenches. Lines of continuous trenches.

Wire. Dugouts. Trenches. Trenches. Wire. Dugouts. How close he was to the border.

July 19: St. Marnier. He built a bridge that crossed a narrow stream. I looked down at it. I couldn't understand its importance. How it could reinforce their position. On either side, dense foliage. Up ahead a deserted village. So much I didn't understand. He would tell me though, wouldn't he?

In Pexonne, he wrote: A few miles from the Alsatian front. How far from the river? From Brissac? He carried the compass with him. He said, This is the Quiet Front.

I repeated those words back to him. I said, Yes. It is the Quiet Front.

He didn't hear me.

We'll be leaving here soon, he said.

He lay down in the field of grass in front of a stream. It was late afternoon.

I sat down on the grass next to him. I wanted to remember the sound of this place.

Would he see this again? Would he think it again? He closed his eyes. What he heard—the sound of birds. The flowing water. The deep green sound of the woods. The birdsong that he wanted to remember. That he would want to remember. Before he left. Before he began the march to the next front.

I returned to 36 via Léal. I rang the doorbell. At first nothing, then the door clicked open. The dark hallway led to an elevator. The elevator opened and a woman emerged. It was Iris. She smiled. She walked toward me and held out her hand. So glad you came, she said. I'd hoped I'd see you again. Come upstairs. We'll catch up.

I followed her into the antique iron elevator that went up to her floor.

She said, It's simple here. But I love it. I travel a great deal, so I don't need much. But I can't seem to find room to put everything.

The apartment so contrasted with her perfectly coiffed presence. The dining table was filled with papers. With file folders. Boxes lined the walls. Above the boxes—photographs, drawings.

I know, she said. Crazy. I'm going to organize this one day.

Of course, I said, I understand. Lately I've been traveling so it's odd to have so little that I need to worry about.

Freeing? she asked.

In some sense, I said.

I believe you came here a few days back? My neighbor told me a woman was looking for me.

Yes.

I travel so much, she said. The neighbor keeps watch for me. I appreciate that. She said, Let's sit down.

She led me to a small kitchen table that looked out over the street. She opened the window. Let me know if it gets too hot, she said. I can turn on the fan.

Wine?

I smiled. That would be lovely.

She took a bottle of wine out of the refrigerator. I'm sure you've tried the wine here by now.

I have. It's wonderful. Dry. Unique.

The island is unique. The volcanic soil gives so much to everything it grows.

You're from here? I asked.

Long story. She opened the bottle and poured us each a glass. She brought out a bowl of nuts.

I'm sorry I don't have much to offer you. I got back late last night. Usually my neighbor will bring me something—fruit, eggs. But she's getting older. No doubt she'll show up later.

This is perfect, I said.

And you? You're settled? Somewhat?

Somewhat, I said.

In a hotel?

Not far from here. It's clean. All I need.

We'll find a place for you.

I didn't answer.

She said, I'm from here. And I'm not from here.

Meaning?

My father was an artist. She pointed toward the living room—to the far wall above the couch.

I couldn't quite make out the image. It seemed similar to the portrait of the woman that Eliade had filmed.

Please go look.

She stood up. I followed her.

Above the couch was the image of a woman with dark hair—parted on the side. She stood in front of a red doorway—against a blue background.

I looked at Iris.

She smiled.

Yes, she said. He was a wonderful artist. He had a promising future. Well, she said, we can't go back. He is a wonderful artist. His work will endure.

I said, I've seen this image. Just a few days ago—in a film.

I see, she said.

Who was he?

He and a group of artists came here seeking refuge—at the start of the war. They saw it coming. The persecution of the Jews. Their art was deemed degenerate. They formed a group. An association.

All painters?

Mostly. There were writers—poets, novelists, musicians. An artists' colony of sorts.

I heard something about that. From a man I met in town. A filmmaker.

Eliade? Yes. He came later. Much later. This island has always attracted artists. I imagine you saw this painting in his film.

Yes.

She looked back up at her father's painting. It's the only piece I have left from him. It's precious, she said.

Beautiful. Enigmatic. Who was the woman?

I don't know, she said.

And your father?

Taken away.

I see.

My mother had already left him. Left the island. She took me with her.

So you were born here?

Yes.

Were you in hiding?

My mother wasn't Jewish. She went back to her family. But I believe she always loved him.

And you?

I was very young. I don't remember the time.

Of course.

I've done this for him. For all of them.

You're not afraid?

242

I can't be.

You knew what I was looking for?

I guessed.

And the pottery? The pottery you export? She laughed.

I see, I said.

You've come here for a reason.

I suppose for the same reason as everyone else here.

She said, Let's sit. I'm very tired.

We sat on the couch below the painting. The room was mostly dark except for the light emanating from the kitchen window.

I said, I've been looking for a woman, a woman named Brissac. I tried to find her in the village when I met you.

And why her?

I went over to my bag, pulled out my notebook and showed her the small clipping that I carried with me. After my mother died, I found this clipping in her armoire. I don't know. I don't know why. I had to find this woman.

Iris took the clipping. Read it. Yes, she said. She was the last. The last Jew left in her village. The village where I met you—in the bar of the hotel.

I was in the right place, then, I said. The Brissacs' village.

She survived the war, then returned. She wouldn't leave. It was her home.

She's still there?

No. Gone. Passed away a few years ago.

I couldn't respond.

She handed me back the clipping. She put her hand on mine. I understand how you must feel, she said.

It's difficult, I said. It became my mission. It drove me.

Like me, she said. What drives me.

I imagine.

She said, Not all is lost. It's been important. And you've arrived somewhere safe, she said.

But they took your father away.

She nodded.

Are we really safe?

I have to believe so, she said. We can do what we want here, say what we want. We can be artists.

I closed my eyes. Pulled my hand away from hers.

Madame Brissac's daughter, Sophie, she said.

Her daughter?

Yes. She's here. I brought her here. About a year ago. So maybe you have found her, her mother, in some sense.

Where? I asked. Where is she?

Not far from here.

Can I meet her?

You will, I imagine. At some point. But she keeps to herself. I can contact her. I'll try.

Iris told me that Sophie often spent early mornings at a beach next to the rock jetty. From there, she walked up the steep steps to town, passing by the open-air shops, fruit and vegetable vendors—the flower market—the fish market.

Iris said that she might not want to speak to me. She may remain silent.

Sophie waded out into the sea. Stood there in the shallow breaking waves. Children splashed in the water nearby. She appeared as I had imagined her. Perhaps a bit older. From this distance. She was elegant—the way she moved across the sand. She swam out past the jetty. To the open sea.

She returned to her towel on the sand—closed her eyes. An unopened book beside her. I stood at the sea wall waiting. Cars honked as they passed. I did not move. I did not want to lose sight of her. I imagined she woke up when she heard the sound of the ferry docking in the near distance. She sat up, took a kaftan out from her bag and put it over her bathing suit. She put the book in her bag—shook the sand from her towel, folding it. She walked up the stairs, past the shops and through the white portico that led to the center of town.

I had come to believe that the island described the exile of the body. This portico she walked through—this portico from where she entered—a space that only movement could describe.

How I tried to describe that moment—as though description would enable me to define place.

There was something about that passage I had to describe. To define the image itself. As though that image of her in that passage would allow me to understand myself.

I made lists of words: corridor, lane, alley, arch. Taking measurements, redefining locale—the geometry of space. Defined by a white stone arch. A representation of that moment.

Place is imagination—the mind—a landscape. And at night, I dreamt of cerulean blue—each image redefined the relation of shapes. The dream read as a page of a poem—lines, angles—typography falling beneath the image the blue darkened.

I continued to return to that moment, to that passage, isolated in the silent corridor outside the square's intersection.

I followed Sophie through the portico to the center of town. She stopped at the newsstand, purchased a paper, then sat down at a table in the café under the sprawling ash tree. Maria came out, brought her an espresso.

I sat down at the next table—afraid to speak.

Maria brought me a café and a water. She said, Will you be here tonight? The festival begins.

I don't know, I answered. Yannis told me he was tired. He might want to stay in.

I understand, she said.

Sophie didn't look up from her paper. Though I knew she sensed my presence there.

I took out the map. Was it meaningless?

The map delineated the space between us. Hours disappeared into breath. I had set up a grid to establish a link between the patterns I had seen.

The space we inhabited—the boundaries of reality.

The Sumerians—their boundaries of reality—how they could depict that in the language of the map. They drew seven islands to hold together the cosmos— unifying chaos—seven realms of uncharted territory— seven days unifying time.

I waited until she finished her espresso. She highlighted a few sentences in an article, folded the newspaper and placed it in her bag. She put a few coins on the table then got up to leave.

Why did I follow her? Could I continue? Not then. Not that day. I could see she needed to remain alone.

From town I usually walked the same route home, following the road back to the hotel—often stopping at the point where the white tufa rock established the perimeter of the coast, imagining early sea travelers crossing the vast water—the sea aquarium filled with life. The sense that always—water flows. As I— watching—moved slowly through a tunnel of glass.

This time I turned toward the beach cove. Broken stone steps led to dirt then sand, passing through olive trees, through seaside plants, fragrant shrubs with yellow flowers. I put down my bag and spread my towel on the damp sand near the water's edge.

The beach was mostly empty. A mother with two children sat on a blanket near me. The mother pulled out a bag of sandwiches. She asked each child what they wanted to eat. They didn't answer. She said, Please, tell me. Cheese. Cheese with meat. Cheese with tomatoes. The two small girls giggled. Okay, the mother said. I'll choose for you.

I waded out into the water. At first a slight chill that soon gave way to warmth. The water was clear. Small fish swam near my feet.

What constructs identity? Is it the past—or a past that could have been? The image of Yannis at the helm of the small motorboat, the totality of land, water, stone—his body in awareness of light and reflection.

I held the chart—an outline of the island. The boat rocked with the current. Our bodies covered in salt.

And he asked, How do we fit into this?

I dove into the clear water. I swam as far as I could before I began to fear I had gone too far. I could no longer see through the surface of the sea. Below me darkness. I floated with the current. No one around. With the water, the sound of the water in blurred silence. Absent of—the landscape of fear. The gentle current. The mother and her two children on the sand. The emptiness and the fullness. At each moment. And the sense of displacement within us.

I climbed the path from the beach. First sand then dirt then steps. I reached the road that led back to the hotel. Along the road a wooden gate opened in front of me. Inside, a small garden—hidden. A man held a lemon in his hand—he had just left his orchard—his boots covered in dirt. He smiled. He hadn't expected me to be there; however, he sensed that I needed somewhere to go. He motioned toward me. Come, he said. Come in.

Please. He beckoned me with his hands to come toward a wood table set in the center of the orchard. He took out a pocket knife, cutting the lemon first in half and then in quarters, his fingers dirty with soil.

He handed me a quarter. Taste this, he said. He took a bite—juice on his lips and fingers. He wiped his hands on his trousers. Took another bite.

I bit into the deeply sour fruit.

His wife came to meet him. She carried a bag of plums, peaches, cherries.

That night I went out to the terrace. Aaron and Helen asked me to sit, have a drink with them before dinner.

I told them that I planned to go to town for the summer festival.

Aaron said, We considered it, but we're comfortable here. Sitting on the terrace, waiting for the sun to set.

The first sound of rockets. Lights over the water.

I understand, I said. I told them I wasn't sure I should go either.

You should, Helen said. Music, dancing, fireworks. Maybe you'll inspire us to go with you.

The waiter brought us out three chilled white wines.

How will I make it now? she asked. After I drink this?

We'll help you, Aaron answered.

We each took a sip of the wine.

Aaron asked, Are you married? Do you have children?

No, I answered.

That makes it easier. To come here. To stay here.

I have regrets, I said. At times.

Of course. He looked at Helen. We don't have children. We couldn't.

Helen said, It wasn't possible.

But, Aaron said, we have a wonderful life. Don't we?

Given where the world's going, I said. Maybe it's better that you don't.

We've heard that enough, Helen said. She stopped. Looked over at Aaron. I'm sorry. I understand what you mean. It's just that we hear that so often.

Aaron turned to her, then to me. He said, God didn't want it to happen.

Who will be left? she asked. Who will be left after we're gone?

We finished our drinks, then walked down to the beach and to the path that led to town. We did not speak along the way. Though it was still light out, fireworks lit up the sky above us. The path to town was crowded with families. Cars jammed along the road. Despite our silence, there was a sense of festivity around us. As we approached the village gates, Helen said, I think I want to go back. I'm just too tired tonight.

Aaron said, I'll take you back.

No, she said. Stay. Enjoy the festival.

I couldn't, he said.

Go back with her, I said. I'll be fine. I'll see you at the hotel tomorrow.

Helen came over to me. She put her hands on my shoulders. She kissed me on both cheeks.

I watched them turn around. They held hands as

they walked through oncoming crowds, walking back up the steep hill that followed along the coast.

I found Eliade across the square by the fountain. He held his camera.

He said, I've tried to remember the city I left long ago. I've tried to remember what I've left. For hours, I've stood here filming the café.

Maria came out from the lighted bar, lighting the candles on each table in the square.

In the center of town—next to the café—in front of the fountain—three men lit a bonfire throwing grapevines then herb branches into the fire. The air fragrant with rosemary and sage, thyme and oregano. In the square, in front of the café, a Romani band played music. Guests sat in the open-air cafes, drinking wine, eating cheese and cured meats.

Maria handed me a glass of sparkling wine. For the festival, she said.

I thanked her. I told her that I wasn't sure I would stay.

She said, But you must.

Okay, I said.

I sat down at a table.

Young girls wearing white dresses with yellow flower wreaths in their hair walked together through the square holding hands. They circled the bonfire together. Then followed each other, sitting down on the cobblestone ground in front of the fire, waiting for the show to begin.

A door in the building on the other side of the square opened. A man with an accordion walked out onto the stone balcony. He wore a white smock and black pants. He played Romani music—his eyes closed, his body moving with the music of the accordion. Moving in a space of abandon. No longer here in the space of the square—but lost in the space of the music.

A performer on stilts, dressed in white, with a white painted face, tossed flowers to the spectators gathered around the bonfire. He stopped in front of the young girls, throwing petals to them. The girls giggled, collecting the petals from the ground.

A barefoot shirtless man crouched in front of the fire with a stick in his hand, igniting the stick, holding it in his hands, moving slowly, dancing around the flames, twirling the flaming fire. Controlled and expectant of reaching that ancient tribal source.

Behind him, a barefoot dancer—her hands the appearance of small tree branches—followed the man's slow, calculated movement—waving her arms—holding her hands out—taking long strides—

movements that took on the quality of improvisation. Each finger—another branch, moving slowly toward the fire—lighting each branch—waving the branches in a circular motion before her before crossing over the fire to reach the man. To become one with the fire. To control it.

They danced with each other—with the fire. With the fire they carried in their hands, which became for them an extension of their selves. Revealing their selves. Revealing the selves that found expression in their response to the fire, in their response to each other, in their response to the accordion player's music.

I tried to push Luca out of my mind. The events of that night. Of that spring festival of violent fire. The men with torches. The parade cart on fire. The appearance and disappearance of memory—deep-seated—yet ever-present. And yet, how? Was it not here, too? Though of a different space—a different energy—with the force of life here—regeneration—renewal—here too in the elaborate dance with ancient ritual we could not seem to escape.

Why here? All of us here in this space in this moment. All searching for home. All finding in this place a no-where landscape full of beauty the essence of ritual—the failure of return. To hold fire. To carry fire. The essence of life. Of its beginnings. And the source of its destruction.

Eliade's images of the homes, the books on fire. Wood, metal, stone, paper. The human at its core. To allow it with the desire for creation. Without the need to destroy.

A window opened in the building across from the accordion player. A horn player came out. A woman dressed in a silver gown wearing a white carnival mask hung from ropes. She swung from the ropes, twirling, smiling at the crowd. Landing on the stone balcony. Where she held on to her gown's train—smiling, spinning, waving to the crowds below her. She—the Summer Bride.

The male fire dancer now had two sticks. He and the woman danced around the fire.

Another woman, dressed in a red gown, was lowered down onto the balcony by a rope—on the other side of the horn player. She swung from the rope, just as the woman in white had. The woman in red danced, playing to the crowd—the same slow movements, responding to the fire dancers in the center of the square. Smiling, laughing. The music playing. The young girls watching, absorbed in the moment—the moment that transported them to a new place of landscape and desire.

I was certain that I saw Sophie standing in the corner behind the café. Leaning up against the stone wall. She watched the fire dancers, the two women spinning on the ropes, dancing on the stone balconies. I knew nothing about her. Only that I needed to find her mother. Because of my mother. Why my mother wanted me to find her would never be known. And that when I could not know, still, I had to find her. How could I approach her? She appeared vulnerable. So out of place in this landscape. Here—but not here.

Maria came back to the table with a plate of cheese and cured meats. She said, After this, I'll bring you something special—a nut liquor. We drink it for the festival.

The Romani band started to play once again. The crowd erupted in dance. Men and women. Children. Girls with flower wreathes. The Romani music—the spirit of the space. How to describe that music? The music of a displaced culture. The culture that found itself here on this island.

Dancing in the square—the bonfire lit. The night just beginning.

I sat alone. And—at that moment—I turned around to see Sophie watching me.

I took another sip of the sparkling wine. I had come too far. I stood up. I went over to Sophie where she leaned against the stone wall next to the café. I said, I've been following you.

She said, I know.

The light had changed—still frame—of night—positioning the camera from the length of time to end to beginning. I saw the night escape the irony of existence. It vanished desire—the lens reflected stillness—quiet—the detail of the map—miniature in range—established as story.

Eliade had said, Last night I had a dream that I stepped through a picture frame, entering the image of the landscape.

Evening strollers filled the square. Light setting—the sky—sea blue. The tables in the small square filling—the Romani playing Minor Swing. The division of the night. A thin line disappeared as the horizon.

The square lit, illuminating the fountain half-masked in cloth.

The portrait of the landscape, he said. He held up the viewfinder for me to look at—the images moving, abstracted by movement.

Early that morning when I saw Sophie at the dock, I had the feeling that something would begin that night. The festival that began in darkness—then light across the surface of the sea. Light initiating the festival. Did it always begin that way?

The crowds gathering at the dock. The carnival beginning. Counting each festival each memory. I followed her through the gates of the city.

Perhaps she saw how the night began. Perhaps she stood at the edge of the square, looking through the distance, across the water. The lights breaking over the watery landscape—the men playing the guitars as drums—the sound resonating, the evening in pause.

Time stopped—the beginning of ritual—the annihilation pondered without space and time—we exist in it. The night a sacrifice. Abundant in the last— exile—the structure of loss. The text, the body.

I opened the French doors. The dark night—warm and balmy. In the near distance the outline of the mountain and sea below. Summer now. The shift. The days growing shorter. How long could I stay here and look out at this view? Soon fall—then winter. The tourists would be gone. I would need to begin writing. I wrote.

I took off my sandals and walked down to the pool. Sitting on the ledge, I dangled my feet in the warm salt thermal water. Thermal water. Healing water. The women on the mountaintop standing beneath the thermal waterfall. Luisa had told me about that place. But everywhere, she said. The volcanic water throughout and beneath the island.

I saw her. The woman. The woman standing below the waterfall. Was it me?

A door in the hotel opened behind me. I turned around. I could not see anyone.

Rustling in the bushes. A rabbit emerged. Stood still, looked at me, then ran away.

I closed my eyes.

I felt a presence behind me. I turned around again.

A woman said, I've seen you here before.

You have?

I know you lived here once.

I lifted my feet from the water. Stood up. Walked toward her.

She said, Wouldn't you like to come in? See the house? See where you once lived?

I don't want to impose.

Not an imposition, she said.

I looked down at my feet. They were wet. I had left my shoes on my balcony.

It's okay, she said. I know you'd like to see the home you grew up in.

Thank you, I said. Yes. I would. But my shoes.

She said, Don't worry.

I followed her to the door.

She said, Of course, it looks different. Different from when you lived here. We've had to upgrade the place. Make it more modern. We have many children now. We need to accommodate their needs.

We entered through the vestibule. I looked up. The chandelier—it was still there. Yet the space looked different. Entirely different from what I had remembered.

We've done away with the formality, she said.

I can see that, I said.

Everything was unfamiliar. The light, the color of the walls. Where were the rooms I remembered?

She said, Would you like to see the dining room?

Please.

I followed her to the dining room.

I said, I remember the dinners here.

The family gathered. Aunts, uncles, cousins, friends. The space created, the evening light. The French doors open to the garden. The platters of food. My mother and father in the kitchen together, laughing. I saw them there. There at that moment. The image—flickering.

I looked at the woman who now lived in the house. She stood just ahead of me. She seemed so kind. She held her arm out to me, beckoning me, welcoming me. Wanting me to see the world she had now created.

There was a small table with chairs. Blankets and toys were strewn about the room—the room in disarray.

The house is full. It's beautiful, isn't it? The children and grandchildren gather here each weekend.

I followed her into the kitchen. In it, women, men, and children were busy cooking. Chopping vegetables, preparing meats. Water simmering on the stove. Summer herbs mingled with the cooking vegetables and roasting meats.

I couldn't discern the discussions. The noise palpable. The group didn't notice me. I walked by them, through them.

Nice, she said. Isn't it?

Yes. Beautiful. But it wasn't my home. Not the home I would recognize. It had been transformed.

Sensing my thoughts, she said, We had to make changes.

Of course, I said. Everything changes. Why have you brought me here? I asked.

She said, Isn't this what you wanted? To see this? When I found you standing outside the door, I knew you wanted to enter. To see this place.

I continued to follow her—through the family room, up the stairs, to the bedrooms.

Perhaps you'd like to see your old bedroom.

Okay, I said.

There were twin beds. The sheets rumpled. My desk was gone.

The kids are downstairs—outside—by the pool. Let's go there.

I followed her back down the stairs to the yard.

It was night and a crowd gathered outside. They sat in chairs around the pool. A large screen was set up, and the crowd watched the images on the screen. Children splashed in the pool.

She said, Is it how you remember it?

I couldn't answer.

Are you glad you've come here?

I said, I don't think I had a choice.

Do you want to join us for a bit? Have dinner? Watch the movie? It's a warm night—balmy. Soon we'll turn on the music.

I declined. Thank you, I said, I should get back.

She escorted me to the door.

I stood outside in the night air—in front of the door. It was dark. I should have felt fear—out there—out here—alone in the dark—but I wanted to stand there alone.

I walked a few more steps up the path. Another woman stood in the street, emptying trash into a bin.

I found myself back at my old house. I was confused. It was the old house—but not the house I had just been in. It was next door to that house.

I looked back at the woman standing in the street. She watched me as I turned the handle of the door and walked inside.

The house appeared abandoned. As though it had not been touched for years, for decades. The lights were on—and the windows looked out onto the garden with a pool. All was dark outside. And I didn't recognize this house either. It was not my home, no longer my home. There were aspects of it that appeared familiar. Familiar aspects that I couldn't quite place, couldn't quite account for. I stood in front of the dining table. A dining table. Not the table I remembered from my childhood. My mother's perfume. A wakening desire to be, to become.

The door opened. I turned around.

A man, a woman, and a young girl entered. They were carrying bags.

The man said, You've arrived.

You knew I would come?

Yes, he said. He put down the bags in the corner of the room. His wife and daughter followed him. They remained silent.

The man said, Did you find the housekeeper's small charm—something she always wears around her neck? She believes she lost it here.

I haven't seen it, I said. I've just arrived.

We need to find it, he said.

He began looking through the house. In abandoned corners. The mother and daughter stood still behind me.

I looked down, under the dining room table. I said, I believe I've found it. I leaned down, picked it up. A small coral charm—the shape of ram's horn. Is this it? I asked.

He came over to me. Yes, he said. That must be it.

I handed it to him.

He said, There are other objects here. Just look around. Is there anything you'd like to take?

I looked around.

Well, he said. Is there anything here you'd like—like to buy?

When I looked back at the room, I realized that

objects covered the table, lined the walls, filled each crevice.

I don't know, I said. I don't know what I can buy. What I can take with me.

He said, Think about it. You have a few days.

A few days?

In about a week, this house and the house next door will burn together.

Would the two houses burn into one? One thing, one being, one entity. The life within them dissolved, recreated. The energy transformed, to be regained.

I didn't want to think about it. This. That moment. I continued to write, sitting at the small table on my balcony.

The bushes rustling again. The same rabbit.

I read over what I had just written.

I felt a presence behind me. I turned around again.

A woman stood in the doorway. She said, I've seen you here before.

You have?

Yes. Of course.

Why didn't you say anything?

It wasn't my place.

I've counted on you. Waited for you.

She said, I can't do any more.

Why?

I've given you what I have. It's up to you now.

I can't do it myself.

She smiled.

You've left me pieces—pieces of a life—of lives that I can't reconstruct.

You're here now, she said. Isn't it a beautiful night? Warm, balmy. Reminds you of childhood, doesn't it?

Yes, I said. I held my hand out to her.

She seemed not to notice. She didn't respond.

I said, Please tell me what this all means.

She smiled again.

I closed the notebook. For a moment, the fire— burning—consumed me. I went back into my room.

Sophie agreed to meet me. I received a message from Iris that morning. Luisa had come to my door with an envelope. It was early, quite early. I had not yet opened the shutters. I put on a robe.

She said, This just arrived for you. She held it out to me, revealing neither compassion nor ire. It was as though she were looking at me and through me. And I didn't know how to read her expression, which withheld so much.

I took the envelope from her and sat down on the edge of the bed. I wanted to cry. I wanted to.

Inside the envelope was a card. Iris had written down a time and place. She wrote: She is a kind woman. I hope that you will find what you've been looking for.

I dressed and left the hotel, walking down the steep road past the fig tree to the walkway that led to town. The path was fairly empty, a few cars, the fruit-seller setting up his truck, the early morning haze slowly wearing off. In the distance, the fishing boats gathered.

I found it difficult to walk—as if a force worked against me. This was it, I thought. This is it. I had everything I owned with me—my grandfather's diary, my notebook, the watch my mother had given me. All those objects I had carried with me. And yet, I had nothing.

It was difficult to breathe. Difficult to know, to think about, to feel the nature of loneliness. So many people around me, their lives I carried with me and, yet, so little I could hold.

I reached the top of the hill and arrived at the church. Sophie leaned against the stone wall. She wore dark glasses. She saw me. Saw through me just as Luisa had.

She was beautiful. Beautiful in the way that you experience life. The fragility of that life—of that being. I could tell she didn't want me to see that. So she smiled. And with that, I saw her age. She and I and all of us had lived—lived in the way that was not ordinary, lived, though, in the presence of what we could live. What we had lived. What time in our lives were left to live. And I was both comforted and frightened.

The beauty of this place. The sun, the sea, the way the salt air felt on my skin. The way I wanted to embrace Yannis for his yearning for his love and hate and the way he tried to accept this. Who we are. Who we were. Who we would be. And I wanted to embrace it all—this place, this landscape, Yannis and Eliade, Iris and Sophie.

I approached her. Thank you, I said. Thank you for meeting me.

Of course, she said. Iris told me about you. Told me it was important. She took off her glasses, turned to look out at the sea.

The view is breathtaking, I said.

She said, It's quiet here. Most mornings there's almost no one here.

We stood in that cobblestone courtyard in front of the small white stucco church built on a promontory overlooking the bay.

The waves broke against the rocks.

I said, I had walked through here the day after I arrived. But I hadn't entered the church. The door was locked and then I felt I shouldn't enter.

Sophie said, I'm not religious. I never was. I come here often, though. Almost every day. Strange, she said, for a Jew who doesn't believe. But there's something peaceful here.

We stood looking out over the wall to the water—toward the outline of a neighboring island.

It's quite warm now, isn't it? she said.

Yes. I could see she felt my discomfort.

Let's go inside.

We passed through the tile mosaic arch—reminiscent of the one in Eliade's film. It was cool inside. Just a few rows of wooden benches on either side of the aisle. A small nave in the front.

She said, Let's sit. There's no one here. I don't see why we can't stay.

We sat down on a bench in the back of the church.

She said, Why? Why me?

I said, After my mother died, I found an article—clipped from a newspaper—about your mother—in the drawer of my mother's armoire, placed inside my grandfather's WWI war diary. I don't know why my mother kept it.

Strange, Sophie said.

I know. Though my mother kept everything, this article seemed out of character for her. Placed among other belongings. Letters. Pictures of me. Pictures of her family. Other memorabilia related to our family.

I read my grandfather's diary—as much as I could. Much of the print has faded. Some of the handwriting impossible to decipher. The pages almost too delicate to handle. I discovered the name Brissac written in the margin of one of the pages. And the words: Can't find him.

My father?

I don't think so. It must have been your grandfather.

My father's father. That would be Isadore. Isadore Brissac.

I've tried to piece together dates and places. All the way back to Romania. There are so many unknowns. Had my grandfather known your grandfather, Isadore Brissac, as a child? Before the war?

Not in Romania. The Brissacs—we've never left France.

I've tried to recreate my grandfather's journey from Romania. 1907. How he had left, how he traveled. Most likely, on an open-air boat—up the Rhine to Rotterdam. Perhaps they met somewhere along the way? On the way up the Rhine? In Rotterdam? My grandfather—with his sister Dora—they'd had to wait there—in Rotterdam.

I wouldn't know, she said. I never knew Isadore, my grandfather. He died before I was born. I never heard any story of him leaving home. It's possible. I only know that—after his father died—he had to take care of his family. So, no, he never left Europe.

My grandfather and Dora—they left Europe—leaving from Rotterdam—on a ship—the Potsdam. They went to New York—before the war. Then my grandfather came back as an American soldier. The diary. I held up the diary. The First World War.

Same war, Sophie said, First World War, Second World War. War. War.

It's here in this diary. My grandfather searching for a Brissac. Your grandfather, I imagine.

Are we somehow related? she asked.

I don't think so, I said. I shrugged. I can't know, of course. Well, in the larger scheme. I've tried to imagine their connection. I can't be sure. I'll never be sure. I believed your mother...

Ida.

Ida. I believed she would help me to discover that connection.

Sophie said, Between my grandfather and yours. Yes. And why your grandfather...was searching for—and couldn't find—my grandfather?

Your grandfather—Isadore—he must have fought also. In WWI.

Alsace was German then.

The German army?

What did the article say? I can't imagine.

That your mother was the last Jew.

Yes, she said. Well, perhaps not literally.

No. Of course not. But of that village—of that landscape that she came from.

In 1940, she said, the Nazis declared the region Judenrein, cleansed of Jews. Everyone—from our village, from the villages around us—gone. Deported. Some fled.

And your mother?

My mother's parents knew they had to hide her. They fled. Fled to the south. Hid, working on a farm. A nun took in my mother—she took many in. She was raised in a convent there, schooled there. She was so young. She didn't know, didn't understand. Later, she told me that she used to cry at night. Wonder why her parents had abandoned her.

They were near her?

They couldn't see her, couldn't let on. My mother's father, I believe, was quite strong—able to do much of the hard labor on the farm. I never met him, met them. Never met any of my grandparents. I can only imagine what their lives must have been. After the war, they brought my mother back to our village.

And your father?

My father survived the camps. His parents didn't return. My father came back an orphan.

Your father's father, Isidore?

Perished.

In the camps?

Yes, she admitted. In the camps.

I believe my grandfather had looked for him—as my grandfather worked in that First War—in an engineering platoon—digging trenches. I can only imagine. Isadore. French army? German? I can only try to piece together moments, memories. I've come to believe these memories—even if they are only mine. These constructed fabrications of my desire to know.

I tried to find her, your mother, I said. I went from village to village.

Why?

Some crazy notion—from my grandfather's diary scribbling—Brissac—and my mother's article—if I could find Madame Brissac, I could find myself. Them. The violence.

Your grandfather searched for my grandfather, and he never found him. Instead, he left you a clue in his diary—hidden in the fragile pages of a war. And now, you have been searching for my mother. And, instead, you've found me.

Yes.

And you see that I don't understand.

Yes.

And that leaves you alone.

Yes. No one knew of her—your mother. One night in a bar in a hotel, I met Iris. She gave me her card. Told me that if I needed help, I should come see her.

She's spent her life trying to help those who are displaced. I know the risks she takes.

So now we're both displaced.

You can go home, she said.

I can, I said.

I'm not sure I'll ever know. Know who those people were. My mother and father returned to the village they had come from. I don't know why. I never understood it. How could they have returned? What was left for them? And yet, I want to return.

Why?

I don't know, she said. I don't know now, at least.

Sometimes I think that we believe that we need to belong somewhere. To help create our sense of self. To understand a way in which we can make ourselves whole.

She said, I don't know anymore—why it's important to know where we've come from, to understand that in the context of who we are.

Was it difficult to grow up there? Feeling that?

I left as soon as I could—went to the University. Became a translator.

And now?

Nothing, she said. Nothing now. I find myself in this place I need to call home. But can't. Quite.

The door to the church opened to a stream of bright light. The church caretaker entered, looked around, then left.

She said, I grew up knowing it would happen again. It was just a matter of time.

I said, I always had the same feeling. It's haunted me my entire life. Nightmares of being chased by Nazis.

It was different, different from what I imagine you experienced.

In many ways, I'm not sure I understand what my parents went through. They didn't talk about their experiences during the war. And, for some reason, I didn't ask. Not enough. They were reticent. I regret that now. I regret not knowing more.

I said, I feel the same way. I should have known more about my grandfather—what he went through.

You're pursuing it now.

Yes.

That's more than I've done.

Why?

She said, I imagine some part of me wanted to distance myself from them, from their experiences, from, well, from myself.

I understand, I said.

She said, A few families returned after the war. After some time we were the last family left. Then I left. I was aware that we were different, different from the other villagers. And, at the same time, felt that we weren't. I felt divided. I wanted to stay, yet I wanted to flee.

Did you feel isolated there?

I don't know. I had friends. I had school. In many ways life in a small village has its beauty. But I felt some undercurrent, some sense of distrust. Or maybe it just came from me, my own fears, my own desires to move on.

I said that growing up I'd always been haunted, haunted by images, by writings, yet compelled to understand what I couldn't understand. There were always vague suggestions of anti-Semitism, vague, I say, because I felt those comments, those jokes my friends told me were unaware, were naive. And I'd correct them. Though I never experienced that penetrating fear—that perhaps you felt—until I came to Europe. That was years ago. I lived there. I found myself growing ever more reluctant to reveal my identity. I'm not religious either. Not at all. When I'd lived in the north, I found myself returning to a synagogue, standing outside the iron gates, looking in. I went there many times. I never had the courage to enter. I don't know why I say courage. Maybe the courage to call myself a Jew, to believe that that was who I was, that it was my identity. The gates were locked. I wanted to believe that this place connected me to my home, to my family. Have I lived my life as a fraud—always running, running away from who I am?

Sophie said, There was one synagogue in my village. A beautiful place. Light and stone.

I know, I said. I was there for an art exhibit. The space—the height of the ceiling. The odd quality of art—art that so contrasted with the nature of the space.

So you know how beautiful it is.

I do.

I never worshipped there. If anything, I tried to run away from that part of my life as well. I loved that space. Though I didn't go often. I now regret that.

Is that why you come here each day?

Perhaps.

In many ways this church is reminiscent of the synagogue. The simplicity of the space, that is. Even the arches here, the vaulted ceilings seem less imposing, more open.

She said, Years ago immigrants and sailors came here to pray. Pray when they believed a storm was coming. She pointed to the nave, to the crucifix. She said, Next to Christ, St. Paul of Padua, the Saint of the fishermen. This place was important for them.

And you? I said.

She looked down at her hands.

I said, For so long I've wanted to understand this idea of the crucifix. I've tried to write about it. I've returned to it. I've traveled through Europe trying to understand it, to understand it within the context of centuries of violence. Perhaps I will never understand it. Understand the power it conveys—how it works to unite, to divide. The suffering, the degradation, the solace it gives, the power it holds. What that image meant to the artist who painted it. When I went to see the Isenheim Altarpiece, I began to fear my own passion to understand this. I needed to get away from it. To escape it—those gruesome images that I felt so compelled to contemplate. The violence that gave solace to the sick. Those images made me sick. I stopped. I said, I'm sorry. I don't know why I'm saying this, telling you this.

We sat in silence for a bit.

I turned to her. I said, And yet, it was a nun who saved your mother.

Yes, she said.

And your father?

My father—after all of the other men in the congregation had died, my father used to go every day to worship. There were no longer enough congregants to create a minyan. He went every day. Went every day to worship. He told us it was necessary. His obligation. To continue. Even with no one else left. I don't understand that kind of commitment. As though without him all 6 million would have been in vain.

I said, You're here. You come here—even if it's not your faith. Are you like your father?

She laughed.

I said, Have you stopped working?

Yes. For now, at least. The work I was doing. The piece I was translating. Deemed subversive. One day, a government agent showed up at my door. Asked me questions.

Were you afraid?

She stopped, remained silent for a few minutes.

Had I pushed her too far?

She looked at me. She said, I was. I am. Afraid to open the past to myself to be seen by them in the present. Does it make any difference anymore?

Maybe you'll work again, I said.

She smiled. She said, I'm a ghost. A shadow of my mother. A ghost of the last Jew.

I said, I've had this reoccurring dream about a young girl's diary during the war.

Anne Frank?

No. Another girl. An unnamed girl. After she and her family were taken away, a Nazi came into their house, found it and burned it. Each time I have the dream, I try to save the diary. Try to read it before the book is burned.

Is it yours?

I don't know, I said.

She looked down again.

I could see she didn't want to go any further. We would talk more, I thought. More. There would be more days here on this island. More time. More time. As long as we were here.

I had to turn away. I had found her, but what had I really found? The last Jew? She, her, I, him. Were we the last? Here, now, on this island. In a church on a promontory overlooking the bay. My body hurt. I began to cry.

She said, Let's go for a walk along the beach.

That afternoon I went back to the cove, walked down the stone steps to dirt to sand, following the path through the seaside island flora and fauna. I found a place to sit on the beach under the shade of an oleander tree. I had my grandfather's diary. I had my notebook. When had his diary become my notebook?

It was a warm afternoon. The beach crowded. I had to find a way to integrate myself into this place. Into this moment. Into the moment that led me here.

I opened his diary. Small. I held it in my hand—the size of my palm. Fragile. The pages too delicate to turn. About to dissolve.

The sole connection I had to his past to his present to the sound of his voice that he tried to remember to conquer to leave behind. Who was this man I had never met? Knew through the words he left here. The words my father seldom spoke about. The words my mother preserved. The words—at times—I didn't understand—would need to invent.

This was not the way I wanted to begin. Not the way I imagined he would have wanted his words to be read. It was only—at that moment—the way I knew how. Tomorrow, it could be different.

A peddler on the beach came toward me—spreading out his scarves, his beads, on the sand beside me.

No, I said. Not now.

Look at this scarf, he said. How beautiful it would be on you.

Thank you, I said. Not now.

I touched the turquoise beads on my neck. They were still there.

He noticed my gesture. He said, Okay. I'll be here all day. I'll return. You may change your mind.

The man picked up his scarves, his beads. He continued down the beach until he reached two young girls—where he stopped and recited again—how beautiful they would look in these scarves.

I picked up my grandfather's diary.

Why did he fight? For what? For where—for where we are here—now? For the expectation that it meant something? Something for him? For his family? For the desire to recover the nature of what it had at one time meant? For all those things that at this moment—looking out at the sea—I did not understand?

He came from there. From where—where I've tried to understand we all come from. The same place. The same valley. He was a Jew. He wasn't a Jew.

He spent his youth in the streets. He went to war. I went to war.

He left from there. I left from there. From the moment he saw the cathedral on the banks of the river. Rose, he said. Rose. They—he—the soldiers—I—drank—

looking up from the café on the banks of the river toward the cathedral on the river. Rose. The name, Rose. They laughed. They walked. I walked. They walked through the night. Where? Why? I walked with him. Through the woods. Across the bridge. There was nothing there. Nothing. Looking down from the bridge, a brook—a little water—mostly rocks. The bridge. Once wood, now concrete. Barely a path. This—the bridge—the bridge I had looked for. Six feet long. I looked down. He looked down. It was the time of year. Spring.

West. Moving west. Movement to the next front. He had not seen combat. Not the kind we, I, read about. They had been on a quiet front—relatively quiet. Yet there was the sense at each and every moment that it was there, here, real, present. Now. About to happen. There was always that threat. Always. Always the sense of betrayal. Of the desire to belong and the inability to.

He returned.

He, they, I walked through the night. Walking through the night—cold and damp. Mud. Sludge. Light. A band of musicians led the way. A trumpet, a drum. They led the way in a communal silence—a communal silence led by the strangely articulated sound of the music that led us.

Inexplicable. How he and I could walk that way— through the damp night. With the musicians leading the way. I didn't think I could make it.

They reached the station. Got on board. Knew that it was about to change. Knew we were about to change. He/they/I—to discover what it means to know nothing about what it means. He was a Jew. He wasn't a Jew.

Rose, he thought. Rose. The cathedral in the night—on the banks of the river.

They boarded the train. To the front. What front? From where—to where?

We boarded the train together. One by one on the train. With our gear. And Rose, he thought. Rose. The cathedral in the night on the banks of the river.

I sat next to him. He didn't realize I was there. He said, Where are we going?

I don't know, I said.

He said, I know, a crazy question. All craziness now.

I said, When we return, we'll understand.

I hope so, he said.

Yes. How stupid. How stupid. Naïve. Why had I said it? Trying to create meaning where there is none.

The train moved along the tracks through the night. The need to remain silent. He fell asleep on my shoulder. I didn't move. I didn't want to wake him. He slept for several hours. The other soldiers slept. They slept. Sleeping without sleep. Half-asleep in a dream world of unbelief. And I could not sleep, watching them.

The train stopped in Coulommiers, a small village in the region of Seine et Maine. It was August 10. French trucks transported us through Chateau-Thierry and Fere-en-Tourdenois. We couldn't see much. We didn't know much.

We arrived early—just before dawn. We disembarked. We left the train, one by one, silently. Well, that's how I remember it. We moved in silence, in discrete silence—toward the next front. Toward our next mission.

He said to me, Are you ready for this?

Yes, I said. But I lied.

Yes, he said. Because he knew.

I said, I will never be able to talk to you again like this.

Of course, he said.

But you've come from here, I said.

Yes, he said. And I left from here.

But you've come back, I said.

I had no choice.

But you're a Jew. And you're not a Jew.

He said, I don't know.

But does it have anything to do with what you do?

He didn't answer.

I knew I could go no further. This wasn't the time, the moment, the discussion he wanted to have. It wasn't right. It was an imposition. An imposition on him on the life he was not yet ready to understand.

I was eager—too eager. And not quite ready to understand how young he was and how much he didn't know about his life, his future, the way in which you exist in it—the world—in it—absent in it—and—how he was just one man in an army of men—dispensable— just another man—he/they/I. Too soon, I thought. And he too young.

The next day we were told that we had pushed the enemy back. Our unit was to work digging trenches. Repairing roads. We were near the end, they said. We passed pastoral countryside—passed the arches of an old Roman viaduct.

We hid in a cave two kilometers from the front— south of the Vesle River. On the road between Chery-Chartreuse and St. Thibault. Farmland. We'd be hidden. Out of danger. Even we weren't certain of where we were. That we were in a cave on the road between two small villages. Near the forest, near the river that divided us from our enemy, from ourselves. But out of the heat—out of the humidity.

Two kilometers from the front. Underground. Damp. Confined. Chickens, ducks. Horses. Cows. Animals. Wine. Grain. Bound together. Underground. In the dark. The dark lit by oil lamps. In the next room—the wounded. Cared for and neglected. A few cots. A medic. Most of us not knowing where we were. Day or night. He took out his diary to check off the days.

Images on the ceiling. Cave drawings. Sources of pain and trust. The soldiers before him. Symbols. Stars, half-moons, crosses. Words, names. Towns.

He looked up at the ceiling, the damp ceiling, dripping. I watched him. I wanted to know what image he would draw. What source he would surrender to. What symbol he would leave as his mark. Markers. Only that.

He took out his diary. He wrote: Best friend died today.

But that was the day before his best friend had died.

They dug at night. Under cover of dark. Then returned to the cave.

The enemy discovered them.

Bombardments.

Gas.

Put on your mask, he told me. You remember how to do it?

I nodded. But I didn't.

He said, Put on your mask.

Okay, I said.

He handed me the mask. He put his on. The gas drifted down—always down. We were caught. Trapped. Nowhere to go.

The gas drifted down. Always down—into the cave—onto the men—him/me. All of us. We were trapped. The animals died. Their bodies began to rot.

We took off our masks.

I said, Are you sorry you did this? Are you sorry?

At first he didn't answer. Then he looked up. He said, I did it for you.

I didn't know how to answer him. I couldn't tell him that it would happen again.

He said, My best friend died today.

The cave rocked. We were hit again. The men screamed in silence. We couldn't scream. They would discover us. No one knew whom to trust.

But they discovered us, he said.

Yes.

Will they remember us?

No.

Are you certain?

No.

Why do you say this? Why do you make me feel like I've fought in vain?

A man in the cave screamed out in pain. He ran to him. He's broken his ankle. He needs a medic.

There was no one left. He carried the man with the broken ankle from the floor of the cave to the room where the injured were kept.

He returned. He said, You haven't answered me.

I know, I said. How can I?

He closed his eyes. He said, Too much to ask of you.

I didn't answer.

He said, I know I'm young. I know I'm naïve. I know that someday I will look back on this moment and wonder why I did this. For what?

You had to return, I said.

I left my country when I was a small boy. They hated us. I was angry. Always angry.

So you had to return.

He said, I don't know. He said, I had no choice.

He thought about Rose, about the cathedral on the river. The music leading the men marching through the night. The train. The transport. Digging. Always digging. His constant hunger. I could not bear it anymore.

He said, My best friend died tonight.

The words began to dissolve in the bombardment the gas the putrid smell of decaying animals. The dark and damp conditions. I could hardly make out the words the dates the ink fading the language fading. Fading on the page in front of me. I tried to make out the words. Tried to piece together the moments. Through the tortured syntax of being.

The next day he went out into the woods.

I did not follow him. He told me to stay behind.

I said, I need to go with you.

He said, You can't.

Why?

Because you need to stay here.

Why?

Because I'm a Jew and I'm not a Jew.

That doesn't make sense. I want to go with you.

No, he said.

Why?

I can't tell you why. I just know that you need to remain.

He left the cave and went out into the woods.

He left me alone in the cave. Abandoned. I had no sense of where I was. Or how I would ever find it again. We were somewhere in the countryside, in the woods—two kilometers from the front—south of the Vesle River. On the road between Chery-Chartreuse and St. Thibault. Farmland around us.

When I would return, no one would have any memory of that cave, of that place. Of that moment. I went from farm to farm, into cafés. I knocked on the doors of homes in this landscape. Everywhere I went, I was greeted with the same response: Madame, there is no cave here. We don't know what you're talking about. Look around you, they would say. Nothing. Just farmland. Livestock. Wheat. It didn't happen here.

I knocked on the door of a farmhouse just outside the small village of Chery-Chartreuse. A woman came out. I said, I've been searching for a cave near here. A cave from the war.

She seemed kind. She wanted to help. She said, Not here.

It has to be here, I said. I stood on the green hillside, on the road between Chery-Chartreuse and St. Thibault. I held up the diary. I said, It has to be here. I opened the diary to the page that described the location.

Everything was silent around us. The world green. The sun hot. The sense of having arrived in a forgotten place.

She said, I'm sorry. There's nothing like that here. No cave. Certainly, no cave. I grew up here, she said. Wait, let me get my husband.

She went back inside the house. Her husband came out. He wiped his hands on his pants. He said, I've just been in the back working.

A small boy—maybe three or four—followed him outside.

We stood together on the hillside.

The wife said, Do you know of any cave around here?

The husband looked up—looked at her. Shrugged. He said, Can't be. I know this countryside. He looked around. He asked me for the location.

I said, On the road between Chery-Chartreuse and St. Thibault.

We're here, he said. We're here. He waved his hands around. No cave here, he said. I'm certain of that.

I thanked them. I said, I'm sorry to have disturbed you.

They smiled. The man said, It was so long ago. Even if it had existed—who would be left to remember?

The woman agreed. She said, Yes, so long ago.

I could no longer read the words on the page. They were not his words. They were not mine. The beach was crowded. The sea filled with families, children, parents, grandparents.

I waded out into the sea. At first ankle deep, then took my time. The cold hit my legs, then torso. I dove into the water. The water washing over me. Through me. And I floated there for some time.

CPSIA information can be obtained
at www.ICGtesting.com
Printed in the USA
BVHW070007100223
658260BV00011B/260

9 781956 005615